Pride Publishing books by Thom Collins

I0527712

Jagged Shores

JAGGED ENDS

THOM COLLINS

Jagged Ends
ISBN # 978-1-80250-763-8
©Copyright Thom Collins 2024
Cover Art by Kelly Martin ©Copyright April 2024
Interior text design by Claire Siemaszkiewicz
Pride Publishing

JAGGED ENDS

Dedication

To my family.

Chapter One

"I saw Jerico Osman for the first time today," Mari Quinn said. "On my way to work. He's much better looking in person than on TV."

Despite her casual tone, Andy caught the interest in his mother's eyes as she watched him for a reaction. He pretended to be interested in the events diary on his computer and feigned indifference. "He's always been handsome. The cameras have never done him justice."

"So, you've seen him around, too?"

"No. Not recently. It's an observation, that's all."

Mari held a mug of coffee in both hands and blew across the frothy surface before taking a sip. "I bet he'd love to see you. Why don't you go over and say hello?"

Exasperated, he gave a good-natured sigh, finally taking the bait. "It's been years, that's why — fourteen, if I've got my dates right. We lost touch. I doubt he even remembers me."

"You remember him."

"Because he's famous now. I'm not. There's a difference."

"But you knew him before he was famous. That counts for something."

"You know, I'm beginning to wish I'd never told you about him."

Mari grinned. "Tough. You did tell me, son, and you can't take it back."

Jerico Osman was the only person anyone in Nyemouth seemed interested in right now. Winner of the TV show *Top Cook* and now a celebrity chef in his own right, he was a big deal. Andy had heard that Jerico had taken a long-term lease on a property on South Bank with a view to opening his own restaurant. Like most gossip, the story seemed to have been around for years with little to back it up until eight weeks ago when a top-to-bottom refit started on the property. Soon after, people reported that they had seen Jerico in town, supervising the refurbishments. A new kitchen was being installed, as well as a bar and completely new flooring. The restaurant was due to open in less than a fortnight's time. The long-gestating rumour had become a reality.

The venue was even on Andy's route to work. He walked past it every day. He'd seen the teams of contractors coming and going as they transformed the one-time bank building into a high-end eatery, but he had yet to catch a glimpse of Jerico, an old boyfriend he'd known in his early twenties.

Jerico had indeed aged well. Though they had lost contact, Jerico had been in the public eye for the best part of a decade, turning up on Saturday morning cookery shows and appearing as a guest judge on later seasons of *Top Cook*. He had a massive social media following and had written several cookery books. Andy even had two of them on the shelf at home, birthday presents from his mother when Mari learned of his past connection to the famous chef.

On TV and Instagram, Jerico looked fit, handsome and fun. His cheeky smile was as infectious as Andy remembered, and he had an easy way of presenting his recipes that made even the most complicated ingredients sound easy to use. Jerico specialised in dishes that celebrated his Syrian heritage, and Andy understood that the new restaurant was to be the same.

"You should go over," Mari persisted. "It's perfectly reasonable. As the manager of Quay House, you could say you want to recommend his business to your guests. You might even get an invitation to the opening party."

"And sound like I'm on the make? Scrounging for freebies? No chance."

"He'll be glad of all the customers you can send his way."

Andy laughed. "I doubt he needs it. That restaurant will get all the publicity it requires."

She tutted, putting the coffee cup down to give him her serious face. "Don't you want to see him again? Aren't you just a bit curious?"

"I'm sure I will see him. Nyemouth is a small town. But I think he'll be too busy right now. He's got a lot going on, and I don't want to push in looking like a nosey local."

"But you're not. You already know him."

"*Knew* him," he corrected. "And a long time ago. He'll probably think I'm desperate or looking to get something from him. I'd rather that we ran into each other casually. Or I'll go for a meal sometime when the initial interest has died down. That could be a good way to reconnect."

She grimaced. "You told me you liked him."

"I *did* like him. But we were barely more than kids when we knew each other...in our early twenties. There's no reason for us to have anything in common now. He might be in a relationship, for all I know. Then how pathetic will I look? The sad ex-boyfriend hoping to pick up where we left off..."

"He's single," Mari said.

"And you know this *how*?"

"I've been stalking his socials. There's no mention of a partner, and I've gone back through a whole year of posts."

Andy shook his head. "That doesn't mean there isn't someone. Not everyone lives their live on Facebook, you know."

"Celebrities do. I should know."

His mother was once the front woman for a dance band in the mid-1990s and had scored a handful of top-twenty hits. Though she was now his part-time events planner, she still had a decent side-hustle going with weekend club-nights and themed gigs around the UK. A couple of times a month she would put on her glitzy outfits, belt out her hits and relive her fifteen minutes of fame with crowds of people buzzing on beer and nostalgia. The celebrity world had changed beyond recognition since Mari had her moments on *Top of the Pops*, but she still considered herself part of the crowd.

"Why don't *you* go over and introduce yourself?" Andy said. "I'm sure he'll find a table for Nyemouth's resident dance diva."

Mari tutted and went back to her coffee. "You're the one he'll be excited to see...not your mother."

Mari meant well, but her constant matchmaking could be a drain. Andy was thirty-seven, and she seemed to be on a mission to get him married off before forty. He didn't share her eagerness. He'd come close to marriage several years ago, but after eighteen months, he'd discovered his fiancé had been shagging around behind his back the whole time they were together. Since then, he'd had no desire for another serious relationship.

"Can we get back to work?" he said, keen to change the subject. "Let's go through the diary for next month. Have the outstanding balances been paid on these weddings?"

It was hardly the most exciting task, but it succeeded in getting Mari's mind off his love-life.

It was early June, and the summer season was looking like it could be one of their best. The hotel was fully booked for the weekends all the way through until October, with very limited availability mid-week for that period. The function side of the business was also at capacity, with weddings, engagements and birthday parties. There was even a three-day sci-fi convention booked in for late July. It was already shaping up to be one of the busiest seasons ever.

It was also one of the most stressful.

Like every other hospitality business in the area, the staffing levels at Quay House had not recovered from the combination of the pandemic and Brexit. Recruiting and retaining staff was the biggest headache he faced in the management of the hotel. They were currently short on bar staff, housekeeping, waiters, a kitchen porter and a sous chef. While all these upcoming events were marvellous for the turnover, he didn't have enough staff to meet the service level required.

"You don't fancy a shift in the restaurant this Saturday, do you?" he asked his mother. Mari had been worth her weight in gold these last few years. As well as doing her own job to the highest standard, she was always willing to help him in other departments when the need arose—be it in the bar, the kitchen or housekeeping. She could turn her hand to anything.

"Sorry, hon. I would, but I've got a gig in Leeds. It will pay a lot more than you do."

"No problem. It was just if you were free."

"You desperate again? I can ask Bev next door. She might be available."

"Thanks, Mam. That would great." He pushed his chair away from the desk. "I'll tell you something. I hope Jerico isn't offering to pay his people too much over the standard rate. I've got a hard time holding on to staff without my rival poaching the ones I already have."

Mari's eyes widened. "Well, if you went over and spoke to him, you could find out his plans for yourself. A sort of *Sleeping with the Enemy* deal. Find out what' he's paying them and offer more."

Andy couldn't stop from laughing. "God, you never stop, do you? Nice try, but no."

* * * *

Andy ended up working late that evening. His deputy manager Sheila had found someone interested in the sous chef job and arranged a hasty interview before the candidate could change their mind. Andy and Sheila had interviewed the applicant, a local lad called Ste, along with the head chef Andrea. Ste had recently lost his job when the restaurant he worked at went bust. He was eager, experienced and perfect in every way. Andy offered him the job there and then, and he could start the next day.

One problem solved.

If only everything in the hotel was so easy.

He was further delayed by an issue with a guest in one of the smaller rooms who didn't believe the accommodation was up to standard and was clearly haggling for a free upgrade. Andy explained that the hotel was full, and there was nowhere else to put them. He arranged for a bottle of Prosecco to be delivered to the room as a sweetener before instructing the staff on reception that no matter how much the man complained, no further freebies were to be offered. Andy had been in the hospitality industry for long enough to spot a grifter on sight.

He never gave in to the extortion of leaving a bad review on Trip Advisor, no matter how much power the guests seemed to think it gave them.

He finally left the hotel at ten minutes to seven, nearly two hours after his shift was due to end and after almost twelve hours on duty. Thank God for his neighbour Jacob, who would have called in to feed his cat Patches that afternoon. Andy loved his job but tried not to let it rule his life. He believed in hard work but also in taking proper time off. An eight-hour day had become a thing of the past in the era of staff shortages and recruitment crises.

But he was done for now. He stepped out of the front door and breathed a sigh of relief.

It was a stunning June evening, with the sun still high above the town and the skies as blue as sapphires. A light breeze coming off the sea kept the temperature from getting too hot and sticky. The town was buzzing with tourists. The beer garden at the front of the hotel was full, while the harbour was lined with people enjoying ice creams and takeaway fish and chips.

Andy unfastened his tie and stuffed it into the inner pocket of his jacket, already looking forward to ditching the suit. A cool shower, a fresh pair of shorts and a T-shirt and he would be ready for a beer in his front garden before dinner. On evenings like this, his house on South Bank, looking down on the town, was the perfect spot to relax and soak up the last of the day.

He picked his way through the crowds and crossed the bridge to the other side of the river. The faces of the tourists, suntanned and happy, proved what a great day it had been. Andy had spent most of it inside Quay House, only venturing out for twenty-minutes to grab some lunch, but it was easy to share the joy he saw all around. Nyemouth could be cold and bleak through the winter months, but in the summer, there was no place better.

On the other bank, the narrow streets offered shelter from the glare of the sun, but it was just as warm. The modern development of bars, takeaways and restaurants along the marina were packed. The Lobster Pot appeared to have a queue of people waiting for tables. The Seagull Café had recently obtained a liquor licence and extended its opening hours. While it served fresh, local food by day, on an evening it transformed into a high-end cocktail bar with live music. It was fantastic to see everywhere doing so well and the tourist trade bouncing back.

The town and its residents needed it.

And they were about to get something new.

As Andy rounded the corner onto Pier Street, he came upon the venue for Jerico Osman's new restaurant. The grand four-story building, standing detached between two terraces, was one of the oldest in Nyemouth. For most of Andy's life, it had housed a bank and building society. It had been empty for over three years since the closure of the bank. As a Grade II-listed building, there was little-to-nothing that could be done to the exterior, but from the construction teams that had been working over the last few weeks, filling skip after skip with rubbish, the interior must have been gutted.

The renovation work appeared to be done for the day. There were no vans parked out front, and the doors were closed.

He would never admit it to Mari, but Andy's interest had been piqued after the conversation with his mother. There was no hope he would ever rekindle that old romance with Jerico, but Andy was interested in what he'd done to the inside of the building. *Purely professional*, he told himself, edging towards the window.

The panes of glass were dusty, and he had to press his face close to see beyond his own reflection.

Shit. There he was.

There were two men on the far side of the empty room, dressed in suit pants and open-necked shirts. Even after fourteen years, Jerico was unmistakable. He was a little thicker than before, broader in the chest and body. He had a neat beard now — that was different — but his hair was thick, curly and short, just as Andy remembered. The light brown skin, broad face and wide, sensual mouth? Andy would know them anywhere.

Andy's face flushed. He was sure he could hear his pulse beating faster — familiar sensations…all so familiar and all entwined in his memories.

He would never have imagined that seeing Jerico again would provoke such an instant and profound reaction. In just a few seconds, he was the twenty-three-year-old kid who had been in lust with the man all those years ago.

My God, he's still got it, more than he ever did.

Just as suddenly, Mari's voice was in his head, urging him on, and before he knew what he was doing, Andy knocked on the door.

Chapter Two

Jerico Osman looked around the empty shell that would soon become a restaurant with a combination of excitement and terror. The grand opening was just eleven nights away, and the place was nowhere near finished. The carcasses of the kitchen units had been fitted but were missing counter tops, sinks, ovens, hobs and dishwashers. The main dining room fared a little better. The floor had been levelled and the walls skimmed, but they were still awaiting carpets and decorations. Construction of the bar had started today and had a long way to go.

"We haven't given ourselves enough time," he said. "We're never going to finish all this."

Rafiq Sultan, his business partner, let out a long, frustrated sigh. "For the millionth time, everything is on schedule."

"We've got staff starting work on Monday. We can't train them on a building site."

"It'll be ready. Relax, won't you? Just concentrate on your own side of the business and leave the project management to me. The decorators begin tomorrow and will take two days. Then the carpets go down after that."

"We still don't have a kitchen. What am I supposed to cook on?" He caught the rise in his voice on the last few words, the note of mild hysteria.

Rafiq smiled, completely unruffled. "It will be finished by the end of the week. There's nothing to worry about."

Jerico forced himself to take a deep breath—five counts in, five counts out. Rafiq was right. He knew it. Everything Rafiq had arranged had gone to schedule. His concern was unwarranted, but as the project came closer to completion, he found it harder to stay calm. This was a big deal...the biggest of his life, more so than winning *Top Cook*. Back then, he'd had nothing to lose. Cooking was a passionate hobby, and he'd applied for the TV competition as a bit of fun, with no bigger aspiration than learning some new techniques. This was different. His reputation and his own money were tied up in the business. Failure would cost him almost everything.

"You're sure these guys are reliable? The contractors?"

"They've done the job so far, haven't they?" Rafiq elbowed him gently in the arm and grinned. "I had no idea you were such a worrier. Focus your attention on something you *can* control. Are all the orders in place with the food and beverage suppliers? Cause we won't have a restaurant if we don't have something to serve."

Jerico nodded. "Yes. Everything is sorted there." Some of the tension left his shoulders. "Sorry. I keep getting swept up in these mild moments of panic."

"You need to unwind. Come on. There's nothing else we can do tonight. Go home, relax and try to take your mind off it for a few hours."

Jerico nodded agreement when there came a knock at the front door.

"We're not expecting anyone, are we?"

Rafiq shook his head. "Not tonight. The contractors are done for the day."

Jerico pulled the bundle of keys from his pocket and crossed the wide, empty floor. "It might be someone looking for work." He would be glad if it was. Though they had recruited enough staff to run the kitchen, they were short on front-of-house servers. He'd even put a sign in the window advertising their recruitment opportunities. He was willing to pay well above the minimum wage for the right candidates.

He opened the door expecting to find an enthusiastic young hopeful, not a handsome man in his mid-thirties dressed in a smart navy suit and an open-necked blue shirt. He looked more like a sales rep than a job seeker.

The man looked him straight in the eyes and grinned nervously. "Hi."

There was something instantly familiar about him — wide eyes, warm and chocolatey, classic good looks, like an old-fashioned Hollywood idol, dark brown hair, parted on the left and swept back in thick waves. He had sideburns and a sexy stubble.

"Hi," he replied, instinctively sucking in his gut and broadening his chest. The man was so damn hot, Jerico couldn't help returning a massive smile. "Do we know...? Wait a minute...Andy?"

The man gave a bashful shrug. "I wasn't sure you would recognise me. It's been a long time."

Jerico rushed forward. "Oh my God." He wrapped his arms around him and drew him into an impulsive hug.

"Oh." Andy laughed, before leaning into the embrace.

The impression of his body, the scent of his hair and aftershave, crashed Jerico into a time hole. The years disappeared, and he was suddenly twenty-four-years old again, carefree and living his best life. When he'd worked at sea, he'd had the most amazing time with this very man. Andy.

Jerico finally released him. "Sorry," he said, abashed. "Was that too much?"

Andy's cheeks had coloured red. "No. Not at all… It was a better reception than I expected."

"I can't believe it's you. Wow. What are you doing here?"

"I live here. Well, up there," he gestured up the hill, towards South Point cliff.

"You do. Oh my God, I had no idea. It's been, what? Fifteen years?"

"Fourteen, I reckon. Thereabouts."

"And how long have you lived here?"

"All my life, really. I grew up in Nyemouth. I moved away for work but came back for good around seven years ago."

Andy Quinn had been one of the kindest, most easy-going boyfriends Jerico had ever known. They had drifted apart when their work had taken them in opposite directions, but he'd always remembered and thought fondly about him. "You know, I kept wondering what happened to you."

Andy shrugged. "I came back here."

Jerico realised he was still grinning like an idiot. He took a deep breath. "I wish I'd known sooner."

"I'd heard you were opening this place. Do you live here, too?"

"I've got a flat on the other side of the river. A six-month lease for now, until I see how the restaurant turns out. But all being well, I'll be looking for somewhere more permanent after that."

"There can't be much doubt about it," Andy said. "The restaurant doing well, I mean. With your reputation and all, it's bound to be a success...guaranteed."

Jerico raised two crossed fingers. "Here's hoping." He roved his gaze over Andy. It was so strange. In many ways he was the same as when he'd known him, only somehow even better, more good-looking. He'd been skinnier back then and had filled out. The extra weight and size suited him. And his face, with fine character lines around his eyes and mouth, was even more attractive. Maturity agreed with him. "Why didn't you drop by sooner?"

"Oh, well, I thought you'd be busy. And I didn't know that you'd even remember me."

"You've got to be kidding."

"And if I'm honest, it was my mother's idea. I think she fancies a meal here after you open, and she encouraged me to call on you. I was going to wait until you were up and running and had more time."

"Your mum is welcome anytime. It sounds like I have something to thank her for."

Andy laughed, crinkling his eyes. "Please don't encourage her. She doesn't need it."

Jerico couldn't stop himself from reaching out to touch him again, a hand on his arm, just to prove he was real. "Come in. Let me show you what we're doing. It's a mess at the minute, but I'd love you to see it."

"Thanks. That would be nice. I used to come here with my mam when I was a kid. This was the main bank in Nyemouth back then." Andy stepped inside, and his eyes widened as he looked around, taking it all in. "Wow. You've totally gutted the place. I barely recognise it, apart from those stairs."

A wide staircase curved from the far right of the room to an upper mezzanine level. "Yeah, that's about the only thing we kept. There'll be a separate dining room on the balcony for when we get busy, also available for private bookings."

"This was all separate rooms," Andy said, looking it over. He pointed across the floor. "There was a counter there and offices on that side."

"All gone," Jerico said proudly. "The walls were just partitions. None of them were weight bearing, so we got rid of the lot."

"When do you open? Next week, right? Will you be ready in time?"

"Huh, that's the million-dollar question."

Rafiq came through from the kitchen. "We'll be ready. By this weekend, you won't even recognise the place."

Jerico made the introductions. "Andy and I go way back. We used to work at sea together."

Rafiq shook Andy's hand. "Please to meet you. Did I hear you say you live in Nyemouth?"

Andy nodded. "Less than a five-minute walk up the hill from here. And I work just across the river. I'm General Manager at Quay House, the big hotel on the front."

"You are?" *Shit*. Jerico had taken over the tenancy of a flat three weeks ago and had been living here ever since. Andy had been under his nose the whole time, and he'd not had a clue. "You should have dropped by sooner. I wish you had."

"You've got a lot to do. I didn't want to get in the way. But it is good to see you."

Something inside Jerico lifted. "It's wonderful to see you."

Rafiq, seeming to sense the mood, stepped back. "I'm just going to get my stuff together. I'll leave you to it." With an apparently knowing wiggle of his eyebrows, he retreated to the kitchen.

"I mean it," Jerico said, lowering his voice. "I've often wondered what happened to you. I tried to find you a few times on social media over the years, without any luck."

"I not really active on those things. I have an account for the hotel, but I only use it to promote our special offers or advertise for staff. I don't do the personal stuff. But I have followed your career. It's been hard not to, as you're on TV all the time."

"Ha. It probably just seems that way. I'm really not. They sometimes record stuff months in advance then they all seem to come out together."

"Even so, you've done amazingly well. I'm proud of you. I never saw you as a chef, though. There was nothing to suggest you were into food when we were together. If you'd turned up on *X-Factor* or *The Voice*, that would have been less surprising. Do you still sing?"

"Only for fun. I haven't done it professionally in years. It was all the travelling that got me into food — trying the cuisine of different cultures, you know."

Another of those devastatingly hot smiles. "I sure do."

"When I returned home, I wanted to learn more about the food of my own heritage. Growing up in Manchester, I wanted to eat burgers and pizzas like all the other kids, but I think the time away gave me an appreciation for the food my family loved. It was that which led me to cooking and filling in the application for *Top Cook*. I never expected to win, but when I did, it presented all these great opportunities that I would have been crazy to turn down."

"And now you've got this." Andy gestured to the empty, unfinished room.

"Yeah, it's been a long journey — training, learning my craft, saving like mad. I always knew I wanted to have my own restaurant, but I just didn't know when or where."

"Well, I'll look forward to trying it out once you open."

Did he think he was going to get away that easily? After all these years. Jerico wouldn't leave it at that. "What are you doing right now? How about we go for a drink? There's a place on the waterfront I've been meaning to try. The Fisherman's Arms, is it called?"

Was that a flicker of uncertainty that passed across Andy's face? After a moment, Andy replied, "Yes, it's The Fisherman's Arms. The terrace looked heaving when I came over the bridge, but there's likely to be space inside."

"I'm not keeping you from anything, am I?" Then more cautiously, "Or someone?"

He checked Andy's fingers. No wedding ring or mark to indicate that there might have been one. He wondered why he was suddenly worried. Nothing ever phased Jerico when it came to picking up hot guys, so why was his confidence faltering now?

Because this isn't just some random guy.

"No," Andy said. "Just my cat...Patches." He checked his watch. "His dinner is overdue, but I can text my neighbour from the pub. Jacob will go in and feed him until I get back."

A pet cat. A friendly neighbour. Getting better looking with age. Andy seemed like the perfect man.

"It will be good to catch up," Jerico said. "You've got me at a disadvantage. You know everything I've done for the last ten years, and I know almost nothing about you."

Andy laughed...a carefree, joyous sound. "It won't take long, honestly. My life isn't as exciting as yours."

"I'll look forward to hearing it, anyway. Give me a minute to grab my jacket."

Jerico raced to the half-finished kitchen. He was behaving like an over-excited puppy. So what? He *was* excited. Andy Quinn was the last person he'd expected to come back into this life, and it thrilled him more than he'd ever have thought possible. And Andy lived right here, in the town where he was about to launch his new business. A strange kind of fate had brought them back together.

"Someone has put a smile on your face," Rafiq remarked, keeping his voice soft to avoid being overheard. "I take it you didn't know he lived here?"

"Not a clue," Jerico whispered.

"Someone special?"

"Yes," Jerico admitted. "He was *very* special. But we were young when we were together, life took us in different directions and we kind of fizzled out."

Rafiq handed him his suit jacket. "Then don't miss out a second time. Here, get going. I'll lock up and see you in the morning." He winked and added, "But don't rush in on my account. Take your time."

"Jesus, Rafiq, I've just met the guy again. We're going for a drink for old times' sake. That's all."

"That goofy look on your face tells me otherwise. Get out of here. Have a good time. You could do with relaxing more. Andy could be the guy to help you do that."

Jerico thanked him and returned to the main room. Andy was standing on the other side, looking out of the stone arched, leaded windows.

"Are these original?" he asked.

"We've replaced the glass, that's all. We can't change anything about the front of the building, other than the sign. Not that I'd want to. This place is beautiful. It was gloomy before, but now we've opened it up inside, it lets enough natural light in. And with candles on the tables, I hope the finished room will have a chilled, romantic vibe."

Andy turned away from the window. He seemed amused. "Romance, eh?"

Jerico's cock twinged. Andy was pushing all the right buttons. "Shall we go?" He gestured to the front door.

They had taken two steps from the window when the sound of breaking glass made them spin around.

It all happened fast. A bottle flew through the broken window.

The flash of a fiery rag.

The bottle hit the stone floor, shattering and spilling its content.

The fuel splattered in a wide range.

A fraction of a second later, it went up in flames.

Chapter Three

A blaze of intense heat seared Jerico's face and scalp. As oxygen fed the fire, it increased.

He grabbed Andy and hauled him aside, protecting him from the blaze with his own body. Andy clung to him, and they hurried beyond the reach of the flames. Andy's face was slack with shock.

"Are you all right?" Jerico gasped. "Are you hurt?"

Andy had been closest to the bottle when it had exploded.

"I'm fine," Andy said.

Jerico guided him to the bottom of the stairs. "Stay there."

Acting on instinct, he rushed to the kitchen and grabbed the biggest of the fire extinguishers. "Get the other one?" he shouted at Rafiq.

Rafiq was on his phone, his face incredulous. "What's going on?" he yelled.

There was no time to answer. Jerico ran back to the main room. The flames still burned, though they had reduced slightly. He pointed the extinguisher at the fire and let it loose, spraying the floor where the accelerant had spilled.

Thank God they hadn't had the carpets fitted yet. The bare stone offered nothing in the way of fuel. With carpets and wooden furniture, it would have been a far graver situation. Even still, the smoke produced by the fire caught in his throat, and he coughed and choked as he tried to put it out. Rafiq appeared and turned the second extinguisher onto the fire. He heard Andy on his phone, talking to the emergency services.

"What the fuck happened?" Rafiq asked between coughs.

"Petrol bomb. Someone tossed it through the window. A few seconds earlier and it would have hit us." The thought of going up in flames with Andy was not one he wanted to dwell on.

"Who? Did you see who did it?"

"No. My back was turned."

Half of the fire had been put out. They worked around it, spraying until the whole area of spillage had been covered, and the flames were smothered.

"Shit," Rafiq gasped, his face ashen with shock.

Jerico dropped the extinguisher and ran to the door.

"Where are you going?" Andy asked.

He didn't pause to answer. Jerico burst onto the street, scanning the road in both directions.

A couple in their twenties, tourists, stared at him in astonishment. The woman was on her phone, and he heard her giving details to the police.

"Did you see who did it?"

The man pointed down the side of the building. "He went that way. Took off on a bike as soon as he'd chucked it in. He's wearing a navy hoodie and a face mask."

Jerico didn't wait for more.

The property housing his soon-to-be launched restaurant was a single detached building. He hurried down the narrow street that divided it from the next terrace. He wasn't thinking straight. There was no plan for what he'd do when he caught up with the bastard. He only had to find him. He'd know what to do when he did. If that meant pulverising the shit out of him, that's what would happen.

The next street ran along the rear of the modern marina development and the lifeboat station. There were a handful of cars on the road, and a few more tourists ambling along the footpaths. Everyone wore light T-shirts and summer tops, no sign of anyone in a dark hoodie. The bastard could have ditched it by now.

Jerico rushed to the marina, which was packed. There were dozens of people in every direction—holidaymakers enjoying the long night and early summer sun. Whoever had been responsible for the bomb had vanished. At that moment, the realisation of what had happened hit him. Someone had thrown a home-made bomb through the window. A few seconds earlier and it might have killed him or Andy.

A fifty-fifty mix of fury and dread simmered inside him.

He wandered another twenty yards along the waterfront before giving up. It was useless. He didn't have a good enough description to go on. All the bomber had to do was ditch the hoodie and mask and they could be any of these people. And if they were on a bicycle, they could be on the other side of the river on the way out of town already.

He retraced his steps to the restaurant. Andy and Rafiq were outside, together with the couple who had witnessed the attack and a group of concerned neighbours. He recognised the woman who owned the fish and chip shop on the other side of the street.

"Are you all right?" he asked Andy.

Andy's hazel eyes reflected the bright light of early evening. "I'm fine. Are you? I don't think you should have chased after them like that."

He was right, of course, but Jerico had acted on instinct. "I didn't know what else to do."

"Did you see who did it?" Rafiq asked.

"No. They got away. They must have planned their escape and known exactly where to make for."

"The police are on their way," Rafiq said.

"I'll have it on CCTV," the woman from the takeaway shop said. "My cameras cover the front street. Send the police over when they arrive, and I'll have the footage ready."

Jerico and Rafiq thanked her. When he looked more closely at Andy, he saw that he was trembling. Jerico stepped closer to him, put his hand on his shoulder and looked straight at him. Some of the colour had left his face.

"Are you sure you're okay?"

Andy scratched his stubble and shook his head. "No. Not really. But don't worry about me. I wasn't the target. What…?" he seemed to struggle for words. "Who would do this? Have you had any threats?"

Jerico looked at Rafiq, and they both shrugged.

"Nothing. The bills have all been paid on time. We haven't ruffled any feathers in the community that I can think of," Rafiq said.

"Me neither. And still, someone has lobbed a bomb through the window."

"It's too drastic to be a random act of vandalism," Andy said. "Some of the kids around here might put a brick through your windows or splash paint over the doors, but this is way too extreme."

Jerico groaned. "Fuck knows, but it's the last thing we need." He turned to Rafiq again. "What's the damage? I didn't have time to take it in."

"Apart from the window and the smell, minimal, I would say. It would have been a lot worse if it had happened this time next week, once the carpets and furniture are in, but we've been lucky—if you can call being bombed lucky."

"Guys, I'm so sorry," Andy said. "This kind of thing just doesn't happen in Nyemouth. One of my neighbours runs the café in the harbour. He had paint thrown through the windows a year or so ago, but that was a vendetta against him by his ex-husband. It's not the kind of random attack I would expect from bored teens."

"No," Jerico said grimly. "Me neither." A suspicion had already begun to form—one he didn't want to face and hoped to God was wrong. Andy wasn't the only person he had history with, and if his inkling was proved right, the other person would be a far less welcome return to his life. He turned his attention back to Andy, wanting to block out the negative thoughts, if only for a few minutes. "It hasn't turned out to be the reunion I would have liked."

It was Andy's turn to put a comforting hand on his shoulder. "That's a big understatement, especially after I've spent a couple of weeks psyching myself up to saying hello."

They both laughed at the absurdity. It felt good to let go of the tension, if only for a moment.

Rafiq went back inside, giving them some privacy.

"I'd like to try again," Jerico said. "Go for that drink and a catch-up. Obviously not tonight." He gestured to the broken window. "If you still want to."

"Oh, God, of course I do." Andy's eyes brightened as he answered. Despite everything that had happened this evening, something about him made Jerico happy. It was mad, really, to be entertaining those kinds of emotions after so long apart. They hadn't even been that caught up in each other when they were younger. They had great times together, hot sex, but when their jobs had taken them to other sides of the world, they hadn't made much of an effort to stay in touch.

What was different about Andy now? He was mature, he had a career and a good life in Nyemouth, to say nothing of being heart-stoppingly handsome. Andy had always been a looker, but somehow Jerico fancied him even more now that he was older.

"Well, I live here, and you have your business, so there's no reason not to." Andy opened his wallet and took at a small card. He clicked open a ball-point pen and wrote something on the back. "My work contacts are printed on the front—phone number, email—but I've put my personal number on the back. It's the best one to get me on. I try to turn the work phone off when I'm not on duty, though it doesn't always go that way."

Jerico grinned and handed him his own card. "Just the one number, I'm afraid. Business and personal is all the same, but I'm very good at replying. I've got a lot going on in the next couple of weeks, but I'd love to spare some time for that catch-up."

Andy slid Jerico's card into his wallet. "I'd like that, too. I usually take Sunday's and Mondays as my days off, so how about delaying our reunion until then?"

"Deal."

In the distance, he heard police sirens. They turned to look as the sound came closer.

"Want me to hang around?" Andy asked. "I guess the police will want a statement."

"No, you best get home and see to that cat of yours. I'll give them your details, but I doubt you can tell them anything more than I can. Hopefully the CCTV footage from across the street will yield more answers."

"Okay." Andy slung his suit jacket over his arm. "Well, take care. Let me know if there are any developments. I pray this was just a random one-off."

Jerico spread his arms. "A hug before you go."

Smiling, Andy stepped into his embrace. They fitted together perfectly. The urge to surrender was immense. Jerico wanted to hold him, lay his head on his shoulder and forget all about the pressure of opening a new business and fucking bombs.

At last, they broke apart, and with reassurances of staying in touch, Jerico reluctantly watched him walk away.

Chapter Four

The evening sky had taken on glorious shades of coral and salmon pink by the time Andy reached the row of houses on South Bank Terrace. He had almost no awareness of walking home. He was still dazed by what he'd experienced in the town below. His neighbour Jacob was sitting in his front garden with Matt and Jake from number one. Jacob waved in greeting as he approached, and Andy saw Patches laid out happily on the grass at the old man's feet.

Jacob grinned as Andy walked up the path. "He hasn't had his dinner yet. I've asked him more than once, but he seems content to soak up the sun instead."

Matt and Jake welcomed him with friendly smiles. All three men were enjoying a beer in the evening warmth.

"I don't suppose you have one of those going spare?" Andy said.

"Is everything all right?" Jacob asked. "You look stressed."

"There's an understatement." He told them what had just happened at the restaurant. They listened to his story with open-mouthed incredulity.

"We heard the sirens," Matt said, "but didn't think anything of it."

Jake stood up. "Sit yourself down, I'll be right back with more beers."

Jacob had a small patio area in his front garden, with a glass-topped table and four chairs. Andy took the empty seat beside his neighbour. Patches rose, stretched and rubbed his head against his leg. Andy reached down to gently stroke the cat. Patches immediately began to purr.

"Quite a shock," Jacob said. "At least no one was hurt. A miracle, by the sound of it."

"Surely it isn't some jealous rival," Matt said. "It's not like the restaurant will be competition for any of the current places. It's going to be Syrian cuisine, right? It's hardly going to have an impact on any of the current businesses, unless they're scared of the celebrity chef angle. Jerico's name alone will put bums on seats."

"A petrol bomb seems a bit drastic," Andy said. "It's one thing to trash a rival restaurant on social media or spread bad word of mouth, but to risk seriously hurting someone and going to prison for it? I can't imagine anyone is that desperate. The town is heaving in the summer. There's plenty of trade to go around."

Jake returned with the beers. He handed one to Andy and took a seat beside his husband. The guys had been living at number one for about eighteen months, since buying the house from Dominic Melton. When Dominic had first moved out, he'd used to rent the place as a holiday let. Andy had been delighted when Jake and Matt took over. It was so much better to have permanent residents living there than fleeting visitors. With Jacob at number two, it was an ideal little community.

Andy took a long, slow drink from the bottle and gasped appreciatively. "Whoa, I needed that."

"You're probably still in shock," Jacob said, eyeing him with concern.

"I'm fine," Andy assured him. "Definitely shaken, but I'm okay."

As if seeking confirmation, Patches jumped onto his lap and meowed. Andy ran his fingers softly behind his ear. The cat stared at him with huge, searching eyes.

"Will it set back their opening?" Jake asked.

He shrugged. "Rafiq seemed pretty certain that the damage was minimal." He described the interior of the building, how it had been gutted and emptied. "They've done all the clearance work. I think the fixtures and fittings start going in this week."

"They should think about security after this," Jacob said. "Another incident could prove a lot more expensive than the cost of a night watchman for the next few days."

"I'm sure they know what they're doing."

"This place…" Jake said with a sigh. "Don't get me wrong. I love living here, but if all these tourists knew half of what goes on, I'm not sure they'd be so keen to take their holidays here. Just look at the last few years. That business with Arnie Walker and his son. My dickhead ex-husband. The murders last October, then all that shit with Catherine Caine this spring." He laughed bitterly. "Did Jerico do any research on Nyemouth before deciding to open a business here?"

Matt took Jake's hand and kissed it. "It's not all bad."

"It sometimes feels that way."

"No different to anywhere else," Jacob said kindly. "All sorts of things go on in towns and villages up and down the country that we never hear about. We've just been in the heart of it these last few years."

"We could do with a break. Just one year when nothing shitty happens."

Matt reached across and ruffled his hair. "You're getting grumpy in your old age."

Jake swatted him away affectionately. "Less of the old. I'm not even thirty."

"*Yet*," Matt added.

Andy sipped his beer and relaxed. He loved the way Matt and Jake were with each other. Their love was obvious. They had been through a lot, including Matt getting shot by Jake's toxic ex-husband, but their ordeal had only made their bond stronger. He hadn't thought about it before, but he'd give anything to experience that kind of love for himself. Even when he was engaged to Jordan, the love had been more friendly and affectionate than real passion. These guys were in it for real.

"Will you go back tomorrow?" Jacob asked, bringing the conversation back to the restaurant.

"I'm not sure, maybe not," Andy said. "They've got a lot going on. I don't want to get in the way." *Or bring any more bad luck*, he added to himself.

"I might call in at some point," Jake said. "Just to show solidarity."

Jake ran The Seagull Café in the harbour with his sister Lizzie.

"That would be a nice gesture," Andy said. "I'm sure they'll appreciate it."

The evening sun finally left the sky. Patches rose onto all fours on Andy's lap and stared at him with intent.

"I think someone wants his dinner," he said and received an affirmative meow.

"I need to get to bed," Jake said. "I've got the early shift in the morning."

Jake and Matt said good night and headed home.

Andy ushered Patches off his lap and got to his feet.

"Fancy something a little harder?" Jacob said.

His closest neighbour always had a superb selection of single malt whiskeys. Because he was so well liked and received so many expensive gift bottles, he rarely had to buy them for himself. "That sounds good."

"I'll give you time to feed Patches and get out of your work clothes. How about I call in twenty-minutes?"

"Great. The door will be unlocked, so just let yourself in."

Patches meowed and circled around his legs in the kitchen while Andy opened a sachet of cat food and spooned it into his bowl. "Give me a few seconds. It's coming."

The cat let out a noisy yowl.

"Hey, you could have had this ages ago. You're the one who wanted to sunbathe with the boys."

He put down the bowl, and Patches lapped appreciatively at the gravy before starting on the meat. Andy went upstairs. His bedroom on the front of the house was stiflingly hot. He opened the windows wide and stripped. He hung up his jacket and trousers, applied fresh deodorant and put on a pair of loose chino shorts and an old T-shirt with Sean Connery as Bond on the chest.

As he padded downstairs in bare feet, he realised he hadn't eaten since lunch and was starving. It was far too late to waste time cooking, so he pulled out a couple of slices of sourdough bread and opened a can of tuna. Patches, who had licked his own bowl clean, suddenly became very excited. With wide, eager eyes and his tail held high, Patches rubbed against Andy's bare legs. He chuckled and drained the canned spring water into a fresh bowl together with two teaspoons of tuna chunks and set it on the floor. Patches lapped appreciatively. Tuna and prawns were his two favourite things in the world.

Andy was finishing off his sandwich when Jacob knocked on the front door and entered. "Not too early, am I?"

"No, come in. I'm done." Andy put his plate and Patches empty bowls in the dishwasher and got two whisky tumblers from the cupboard. He also poured a jug of water and carried them to the living room where Jacob had made himself comfortable on the sofa.

"Tough day, then?" the old man asked, taking a bottle of single malt from its presentation box.

Andy sank into his armchair with a weary sigh. "The usual twelve-hour summer shift, topped off by a bit of arson."

"I'm glad you can laugh about it." Jacob poured two hearty measures and handed one over.

Andy added a splash of water to his glass and made himself comfortable. "I'd go a bit mad if I didn't laugh."

"Has the shock worn off? I can see you've got some colour back in your face."

"I'm all right." He took a long, thankful sip. The whisky was wonderfully smooth and oaky. It soothed his throat and stomach when he swallowed. Patches came through, sat at his feet and proceeded to clean his whiskers. "It was weird, being there at that exact moment. I wouldn't have gone to the restaurant if it hadn't been for my mother encouraging me. I was on my way home when I made the decision on impulse to call."

"You say you knew Jerico from before?"

"A long time ago. We worked on a cruise ship together. *Atlantic Pride*, the ship was called. He was a singer, and I worked on the shore excursions desk, you know, selling trips for each port we visited."

"Sounds exciting. I worked at sea myself for many years when I was young. Merchant vessels, nothing as glamourous as a cruise ship."

"I loved it. We didn't get a lot of time off. It wasn't the holiday lifestyle people take it for. We worked for months at a time without a day off, just a few hours here and there when we were in port, but it was an amazing experience. I went all over the world and saw things I would never have imagined if I'd stayed here in Nyemouth. Even did a five-month world cruise. Now, *that* was special." Andy smiled as he recalled those glory days at sea. "Back then, in my twenties, I would never have imagined taking a job back on land."

"So, what brought you home?"

"I missed my family. My grandparents were getting older at the time. I reconsidered my options when I was thirty and decided my days on the ocean were through."

"Is that when you lost touch with Jerico?"

"Oh, no. It was well before that. We got together when I was around twenty-three. I hadn't been working on the ships all that long. It was maybe my second contract—I can't quite recall—but I remember meeting him all right. He came onboard when the current entertainment team reached the end of their term. Jerico joined the ship as the replacement troupe.

He was one of those people who drew you to them like a magnet. It was impossible to resist."

"Entertainment, so he wasn't always a chef?"

"No, he was just a singer back then—one of the best I'd ever heard. There were four singers and four dancers in the team. They used to put on these big production shows in the theatre. You know the kind of thing—Broadway musicals, Abba tribute shows, movie-themed nights. Jerico could adapt to any genre, but his voice was really suited to the show tunes. He had a big sound that could raise the roof when he let rip. It used to give me goosebumps. I was really surprised when he won that cookery show, as I always imagined he'd end up winning *The Voice UK* or something like that."

Jacob's bright eyes flickered at him. "From the way you're talking, it's clear he meant a lot to you."

"He did, but we were both young and excited to be seeing the world. We started dating pretty soon after he joined the ship—and it was hot and heavy. Relationships at sea are not like those you have ashore. You're in this contained space for weeks at time, and your senses and emotions are overwhelmed by all these new places you visit. It's like everything is turbo charged and accelerated. Know what I mean? Within days of getting together, we were living with each other constantly, like a married couple."

Andy took another drink and gazed out of the window. The sky across the bay had taken on a deep, violet shade. It would be dark soon—not that it got dark for long at this time of year.

"Don't get me wrong," he continued. "I'm not saying any of that was bad. The complete opposite. We had a wonderful time. I loved being with him. He made me laugh. I was awed by his talent. And what can be more romantic than watching the sun set over the ocean with a guy who looks like an underwear model?"

"Then what are you saying? You were too young to appreciate it?"

"I think we were, yes. When my contract on that ship ended, I came home for a couple of months before starting a new one, but I was put onboard a different ship. And we were never in the same place at the same time. From living on top of each other, we couldn't have been farther apart. We both moved on."

"And that was that?"

Andy nodded. "Until today, yes. Obviously, I've followed his career. It would have been hard not to, given how famous he's become, but we lost touch. I eventually returned to Nyemouth, and Jerico started his new life in food."

Patches leapt onto the armchair and settled at his side. Andy stroked him gently behind the ear. The cat closed his eyes and turned his head towards him,

"And after today?" Jacob asked. "Is there a chance you could pick up where you left off all those years ago?"

Andy sighed. "I have no idea. I was just getting used to seeing him again when the bomb went off. Jesus, even saying that out loud sounds crazy. After all this time, I don't see how we could. We're different people. We live such different lives. We don't have the same things in common anymore."

"You're making excuses," Jacob chided.

"Maybe…probably." He sighed again. "After what happened tonight, I think Jacob Osman's world is far too exciting for me. Whatever is going on down there, I'm not sure I want to get involved."

Chapter Five

The following morning, Jerico was surprised to check his phone at the side of the bed and discover it was almost eight-thirty. He was not a late sleeper. Most days he got up before seven. Then again, he hadn't fallen asleep until sometime after three. With a groan, he shuffled up the bed, rearranging the pillows behind his head, as the memories of last night came crashing back.

The police hadn't left the restaurant until almost eleven. By the time someone came out to secure the broken window, it was closer to midnight. When he returned to the flat, he had been exhausted, but his mind was too wound up to go to bed. He'd paced the floor, but it had taken three double vodkas to calm him down enough to sleep.

He flung back the covers and got out of bed. There was no rush to get to the restaurant—the project manager had keys—but he couldn't waste a minute more lounging around. He needed to act. Last night he had felt helpless, but today he planned to take control. He went to the bathroom, pissed, showered and got dressed in navy chinos and a pale blue, short-sleeved linen shirt.

He made his way to the kitchen on autopilot. He poured a glass of orange juice, took his vitamins and put the kettle on to boil. He had to keep busy. The situation required action, and he was ready to tackle it head on. The more he thought about the arson attack, the more messed up it seemed. One moment he'd been full of delight, seeing Andy again after so many years, then boom, a bomb had literally blown his happiness apart.

Andy. Christ, it had been good to see him again. With what happened afterwards, Jerico had barely given him a second thought. Opening the door to discover his handsome ex had been a huge surprise. Andy had changed a lot, then in many ways he hadn't changed at all. The boyish twinkle in those warm brown eyes was as familiar as ever…and that winning smile. The years they had been apart melted away while they were talking. Jerico had never experienced that kind of thing before. He'd run into a few previous partners over the years, but the old spark, the connection was always missing, but with Andy, it was like they had only seen each a few days earlier. Jerico had been shocked to realise the affection he'd had for him was as strong as ever.

He retrieved his wallet from the counter and took out Andy's business card. *General Manager, Quay House.* Jerico had seen the big hotel in the harbour. He'd walked past it many times, noting how busy the bar seemed to be. He'd even gone online to check out their restaurant menu, scoping out the competition. The hotel catered to traditional British tastes with steaks, fish and chips, and roast dinners. They had a four-and-a-half-star rating on Trip Advisor and other sites. Customers found little to complain about, but Jerico dismissed them as business rivals. He intended to offer a fine dining experience, a taste of his Syrian heritage. He wouldn't harm the hotels trade and doubted they would impact upon his. There would be room for both of them in Nyemouth. In all his research he'd never bothered to find out who oversaw the hotel.

Andy had done well for himself since his days of selling holiday excursions.

Why should that come as a surprise? He'd always been driven. He regularly smashed the monthly sales target and was always mentioned favourably in the customer satisfaction surveys at the end of each cruise. Even when he was young and out to see the world, Andy had been a hard-working professional.

And here they were again, together in the same place.

How was he coping after what had happened last night? Though Jerico and Rafiq had been the target, it must have shaken him to be involved in something so vicious.

Jerico turned the card over. Andy's personal number was printed in his neat handwriting. *Fuck it.* He had a lot to deal with today, but he wasn't about to sweep Andy aside for the sake of his career. He'd made that mistake once before.

He grabbed his phone, keyed Andy's number and details into the contacts and composed a new message.

Hi. I hope you're okay after last night. It was a shame we didn't get that catch-up drink. I hope we can do it sometime soon. J. x

He considered adding another two kisses but stopped short. It was over the top, considering they had only spoken to each for about ten minutes in total. He sent the message.

There was no time for a fancy breakfast. Jerico took two eggs, butter and milk from the fridge and hastily scrambled them. He couldn't even be bothered to cook them in a pan and set them away in the microwave while he made toast and coffee. His phone bleeped as he waited.

A reply from Andy.

Hi. I'm fine. I hope you are, too. It was a big shock. I hope they catch who was responsible soon. I'm free whenever you are and never far away for that catch-up. Take care xxx.

Jerico smiled and immediately regretted the single stingy kiss on his own message.

What was the fuzzy, warm feeling creeping over him? He hadn't felt anything like it in years. He'd thought it was just the kind of thing people experienced in their youth and that adulthood and the problems that came with it swept those sweet, romantic feelings clean away.

Andy still had the power to trigger those good vibes.

Jerico ate his breakfast at the table. A slew of text messages from Rafiq and friends who had heard about the arson attack soon brought him back down. He was in no mood to reply yet. He knew that people meant well, but he couldn't go through the long process of answering them…not this morning. When he got his head together, later in the day, he would fire off a single message to everyone who had reached out.

He finished his breakfast and loaded the dishwasher. He was about to brush his teeth and get ready for work when the door buzzer went off. Apart from Rafiq, he hadn't had any visitors to the apartment since moving in.

"Yes," he answered through the intercom.

"Mr. Osman," came the reply, "it's Detective Constable Andrea Brown. I'd like to speak to you about the incident at your restaurant. Is this a good time?"

He released the door. "Come on up…second floor."

He unlocked his own front door and was waiting when DC Brown reached the landing. Her cheeks were flushed, and she was slightly out of breath. "These stairs are steep," she remarked.

"Sorry… There's no lift, either." The apartment was in an old four-storey townhouse that had been broken up into individual flats. Though the old-world staircase was impressive, Jerico was glad he hadn't taken a lease on the very top floor.

The detective smiled and showed him her ID card. Jerico welcomed her inside.

"Can I get you anything?" he asked. "Tea? Coffee? Juice?"

"I'd appreciate a glass of water if it's not too much trouble."

Jerico retrieved a tall glass from the cupboard and drew water from the inbuilt filter in his fridge. "I take it you're not here to tell me you've caught who was responsible?"

"If only I were." She accepted the glass gratefully and took a good glug. "It's scorching out there already," she commented, tipping her head towards the window.

"I haven't been out yet. It's shaping up to be a hot summer, though."

DC Brown produced her notebook. "Okay if we sit?"

Jerico noticed for the first time that she was pregnant. He pulled out a chair at the kitchen table and sat across from her.

"I'm following up on the statement you gave at the venue last night," she explained.

"I'm glad you came. I was going to call the station anyway."

"You've thought of something new?"

He nodded. "I've been thinking about it for most of the night. I'm not sure why I didn't mention it before."

"You were in shock. It's natural. It takes the mind a while to process something like this. What have you got?"

Jerico took a deep breath, then rose to get himself a glass of water, too. Telling this story never got any easier. "There's someone you should probably investigate. His name is Dean Ferguson."

"And who would he be, then?"

"I have a restraining order against him of indefinite length. He's not allowed to contact me or come anywhere near me."

DC Brown wrote down the name. "And why is that?"

"Among other things, he broke into a restaurant where I used to work and started a fire in the kitchen. It was a deliberate attack against me, resulting in thousands of pounds in damage and lost takings. He got four years in prison for it. Of course, he only served half of that."

"Do you know where he is now?"

"The last I heard he was in Durham. I used to get regular updates from the victim liaison officer in the Probation Service. They supervised him on licence following his release from prison, but his licence expired about ten months ago, and they no longer have contact with him. At that stage he was living and working in Durham."

She scribbled down the details. "Do you have the contact details for the victim officer?"

He tapped into his phone and gave her a name and phone number.

"You'd better start at the beginning. What made this Dean guy target you in the first place."

Jerico opened Google and searched for the cast photo from his season on *Top Cook*. "Well, I did this TV show about ten years ago."

"I know it."

"In the beginning, they had fifty contestants, and over a course of elimination tests, they whittled us down to ten semi-finalists." He turned the screen towards her. "This is the ten from my year. That's me second from the right, and here" — he enlarged the photo to zoom in on another face — "is Dean Ferguson."

Dean had been a baby-faced twenty-five-year-old at the time of the competition, one of the youngest competitors that season. With his short brown hair and clean-shaven features, he had looked about sixteen.

"I only recognise you from that lot," DC Brown said. "I'm not a huge fan of cookery shows. I'm a takeaway girl myself. So, what happened to him? He obviously didn't win."

"Well, he made the last ten, but in the next round Dean and I had to go up against each other, and I beat him. Dean ended up tenth overall, and he wasn't happy. I don't want to see it again, but if you search YouTube, you'll find the clip of his elimination. Most contestants smile and thank the judges for the opportunity of taking part but not Dean. He kicked off. They only showed part of it on TV but he slagged off everyone, especially me. He said I cheated. He said the judges were biased and fixed the result. It was a big deal for a hot minute at the time. I still see people using memes and GIFs of his outburst on social media. I was even amused myself for a while…but not for long."

"Then what?"

"He made a lot of noise online and gave interviews to the press. But it was a few weeks later when the episode where I won was screened that he really went for it. The fact I beat him in the round then went on to win the competition seemed to trigger something far deeper. He hated me." Jerico reached for the water. He loathed having to talk about all this again. It had been nearly ten years ago. He'd gone through five years of hell until Dean went to prison, and since then his life had been much calmer. "It started low-key enough — slagging me off on forums and Facebook groups, claiming the show was fake and rigged. The producers had to publicly deny all his allegations, which only made him worse. The trolling progressed to actual stalking. Over a period of four years, he harassed me at work, he created catfish accounts to entrap me, he hacked my computer and posted personal stuff online, set up accounts posing as me to dupe people and spread racist and sexist material and he sent letters to my neighbours. You name it, and he did it."

"And it came to a head when he lit this fire?"

Jerico nodded. "I had a restraining order in place against him by then because of the stalking. I already knew he had breached it. We'd get a lot of bookings for diners who didn't turn up. We had to start calling our customers back just to confirm who they really were before accepting further bookings. He'd caused a lot of problems."

"Did he admit to starting the fire?"

"Not at first. But then he lost it while he was under caution and blurted out the whole thing during one of his rants about me."

DC Brown closed her notebook. "He definitely sounds like a person of interest. Have you heard from him lately?"

"Not a thing. He served his sentence, and as I said, he was released early on licence. The victim officer would keep me up-to-date on his progress and whereabouts, but that all stopped with her involvement in the case." He pondered for a moment. "There hasn't been anything in years. The usual stuff he used to do, the trolling and fake bookings, I haven't noticed anything like that. And I got pretty good at recognising his patterns. The profiles used to change, but there were certain phrases that gave him away. There's a good chance it might not even have been him last night. His time in jail might have changed him. He had a lot of issues. Maybe he managed to deal with them."

DC Brown gave a reassuring smile. "That could be true, but it won't hurt to know where he is now and make sure he's not breaching the terms of that restraining order."

Jerico remembered all those difficult days. He did not consider himself to be a victim. When someone came for him, his instinct was to fight back. But Dean's harassment had been so persistent and pervasive that it had worn him down more than once. Life had been so quiet for so long, he'd almost forgotten how stressful those early days had been. Learning a new craft, training in some of the most high-pressure kitchens in the country had been tough enough, without the burden of a stalker.

He hoped the current incident was unrelated, but the more he dwelt on the idea, the stronger it became. Dean had always been jealous of him. Just because he didn't message Jerico anymore, didn't mean he wasn't still following him online. Jerico had posted a lot on his socials about the restaurant and how proud he was to finally open his own place.

Would that be enough to trigger another vengeful episode from his rival?

Jerico hoped he was wrong, but a niggling feeling in his gut told him he was on the right track.

Chapter Six

Andy was in his office on Friday morning and wondering whether or not to send a text to Jerico and ask if he was free for lunch. They hadn't seen each other since the fire incident on Tuesday night but had messaged several times each day. Jerico had a lot on his plate. Andy was more than aware of that. His restaurant was due to open a week from today, and he would be working around the clock to get everything ready. Andy had worked in hospitality long enough to know how busy things could get when a major event was close.

Would Jerico appreciate the distraction of a friendly lunch right now, or would it be a massive inconvenience?

Damn. Why couldn't he make a decision?

Because the situation was complicated. Because he didn't know his own mind or understand his feelings. A lot of time had passed since they had known each other last. It was true, he'd been thinking about Jerico a lot in the past few days. He'd even been checking out his social media to keep track of the restaurant's progress. Naturally enough, there was no mention of the attempted arson on Jerico's feeds, just lots of photos of him posing with contractors in hard hats and making cups of tea for the workers — the usual, bland celebrity updates, but worth checking out for the pics. Jerico's socials were the definition of eye candy.

If nothing else, it was obvious to Andy that he wanted to get to know Jerico again.

The problem was timing. If not now, when? And would there ever be a perfect time? If the restaurant was the success Jerico hoped it to be, he'd be busy non-stop in the coming weeks. And if it took off big, wouldn't he want to franchise it and open branches in other towns, which would mean moving away? Andy groaned. He was setting obstacles in his own way and making excuses — exactly the kind of thing he would challenge one of his friends or colleagues for doing.

His thoughts were interrupted when Mari knocked at the door. The heat inside was stifling, and he had opened his sea-view window and propped open the door in the hope of getting a breeze through the office. The attempt had been semi-successful.

"Hi," he said, putting his phone down. "What's up?"

Mari sat on the other side of the desk, looking pleased with herself. "I've only solved your staffing problem, that's all." She put an A4 envelope on his desk. "CVs. Both looking for restaurant work, both experienced and both available for immediate starts. You can call them in for interviews and thank me later."

He pounced on the envelope, pouring over the documents. "Do you know them? Are they reliable?"

Mari swivelled her chair to face the open window and fanned herself with a brochure from his in-tray. "I know one of them and know of the other. They both come highly recommended."

"So how come they are so readily available?"

"They've been laid off. They've both been working at Sleighly Hall, but it's shutting down."

He gasped. "It is?" Sleighly Hall was a posh country hotel a few miles inland. It was a popular wedding venue with its own deer sanctuary. He'd heard the owners were in financial trouble but had no idea it had gotten so bad.

"At the end of the month...but they have started letting the staff go already. Don't waste any time getting this pair in for an interview or they'll be snapped up by someone else. Your handsome ex with the fancy new business, for example." She gave him a cunning side eye.

Andy ignored her and checked out the potential candidates.

Not to be deterred, she continued, "Have you arranged to meet him yet? The lovely Jerico."

"No." She bored her eyes into him from across the desk. "But I will at some point."

"I don't know why you're dragging your heels on this. I can tell you like him. Ask the man over for a drink."

"I will," he insisted, "when I'm ready. Stop pushing me. The last time I listened to your advice, someone chucked a petrol bomb at us."

Mari swivelled to face him and jabbed a finger on the desk. "That had nothing to do with me — or you, for that matter. It was just a petty little hoodlum. You know what some people are like around here. They'll be livid at the thought of a Syrian business opening in their precious whiter-than-white town."

He put down the paperwork and looked at her seriously. "Is that what you think it is? Racism?"

"Absolutely. Look at the hassle the Polish guys have had at the gallery over the years. And the Chinese takeaway have had their windows put out twice in the last few months. There's always been a horrible undercurrent of intolerance running through Nyemouth. Just because Jerico is a famous chef, I doubt they'll treat him any better. Little bastards."

She had a point. Of course, Jerico would be a target for the hate-mongers. Even if his heritage wasn't a problem, a lot of small-minded, small-town people would be jealous of his success and want to bring him down to make themselves feel better.

"I'll text him later," he assured his mother.

"Don't text. *Call* him."

"Yes, madame. Now, is that all you wanted, because I'd like to call these candidates before they get a better offer?"

"Actually, I came to ask a favour."

"Yes?"

"Are you free tomorrow night? I've got a gig in Leeds. Richie was going to come with me, but he has to work now. I would go on my own, but I feel better having company, especially for the late-night shows."

"Yeah, sure. I haven't got anything planned."

She got to her feet, smiling at him. "Thanks, son, you're a star. I'll do all the driving, and you can have a drink and enjoy yourself. It's just so I've got some muscle if things get rowdy."

Andy laughed. Mari had been singing in pubs and clubs since before he was born. If things got out of hand, she could handle the situation far more effectively than he could.

"I'm on at one a.m. If we leave about seven-thirty, we should get there before ten. We can go for food before the gig. My treat."

"Sure, send me a text in the afternoon to remind me."

She paused on her way out of the door. "And you're going to call Jerico later, right?"

He raised his hands in surrender. "I promise."

"Good. Ask him out tonight, then you can tell me all about it in the car tomorrow."

After she left, he got straight on the phone to the potential employees. He had a good feeling from both by just talking to them and arranged for them to come in later that afternoon for interviews. Maybe things were at last starting to look up on the staffing front. He'd been juggling with shortages for months.

By the time he had dealt with that, it was too late to arrange lunch with Jerico, as he didn't have time. He would call him later in the afternoon and see if he fancied a catch-up drink that evening.

Despite the open windows, the office was still overly hot, and he needed to get out for a short break. He decided to walk along to The Seagull Café and pick up something for lunch. He'd had a delicious fresh crab sandwich from there earlier in the week and could fancy the same again. Leaving his suit jacket behind, he grabbed his sunglasses and headed out. He had about twenty-five minutes maximum to buy his lunch and eat it.

The town was packed when he stepped outside. Friday, officially the start of the weekend, and the tourist crowds had already arrived. Quay House didn't have a single vacancy. None of the guests who had checked in yesterday were leaving before Monday. Most of the horde were heading down the street in the direction of the beach, and he had to fight against the tide to reach the bridge.

There had been a revolt from a minority of residents against the booming tourist trade, something they saw as an invasion. A lot of people had discovered Nyemouth for the first time in the aftermath of the pandemic, when they had not been able to travel abroad for their holidays. And having found it, those same people now returned again and again. As a business owner, Andy embraced the town's newfound popularity, but he could also appreciate the other argument.

The streets had never been this crowded when he was growing up. Nyemouth had been a nowhere little fishing town back then, not a holiday hotspot.

As he crossed the bridge, he saw a familiar face in the crowd coming towards him.

Ethan Bradshaw spotted him, too, and, with a wide grin, changed course to meet him.

"Hey, how are you doing?" Ethan asked.

"I'm fine. Are you?"

Ethan worked at the Nyemouth and Northumberland Gallery. Since the departure of Antoni Nowak, one of two brothers who had founded the gallery, Ethan had been promoted to the role of assistant manager. He was a good-natured, good-looking lad of twenty-six. Somehow, since a random Grindr hook-up the year before, Ethan and Andy had struck up a semi-regular 'friends-with-benefits' arrangement. Blond, blue-eyed, athletically built, Ethan was the definition of hot young twink, which was something of a problem.

Twinks were not Andy's type.

The sex was fun, but Andy had never fully understood how it had progressed into an on-going arrangement. It just had. He suspected Ethan would be open to the possibility of something more, but he'd always been clear that he was not looking for a relationship. It wasn't even an age-gap thing. Though Andy preferred guys closer to his own age, there was only eleven years between them. He just felt that outside of the bedroom, they had no common interests. Like a lot of younger men, Ethan was into social media, reality TV and gaming, and Andy definitely wasn't. Andy liked football and eating out, both of which Ethan found boring.

And yet, they kept hooking up to fuck.

"Haven't seen you in a while," Ethan said with a grin, looking Andy over.

"I've been busy," Andy said, tipping his head to the huge crowds. "You know what it's like."

"Totally. We haven't stopped all morning. Well, we've been rushed off our feet all week. I've just popped out to grab us some coffee."

"I'm glad to hear that. I'm in a bit of a hurry myself." Andy felt like a prize shit, but he didn't have time to stand around and chat. Not today.

"I'm free later," Ethan said, a suggestive smile on his lips, "if you fancy getting together. Like I said, it's been a while."

Andy had been hoping to avoid this conversation. Might as well get it over with. "Oh... Well, that's probably not a good idea."

Ethan's face fell. Andy felt like he was tormenting a little puppy.

"Look," he said, desperate to find the right words for this. "What we've had has always been a casual thing, right? It's been wonderful, it really has, but…erm, well, I might have met someone. I mean, no, that's not right. *Shit.* I *have* met someone recently. It hasn't gone anywhere yet, and it might not for all I know, but…"

Ethan put a hand on his arm. "Relax… I understand. You've met someone and don't want to fuck it up before it's even started."

Andy laughed with relief. "*That's* what I was trying to say…badly. Thank you."

"That's cool. I'm pleased for you, and I hope it works out. He's a lucky guy."

"What about you? No one special you're interested in?"

He widened his eyes in mock horror. "One person? Nah, fuck that. I'm not ready to settle down just yet. But whoever this guy is, good luck. See you around."

And with that, he was gone, merging into the crowd.

Andy gawped after him. How did a man in his mid-twenties have his head so well together? Andy hadn't had a clue what he'd wanted when he had been Ethan's age. *Still, don't even now.*

Here he was stressing and delaying about getting in touch with Jerico, afraid of what might or might not happen, while Ethan had just brushed him off like a piece of fluff on his shirt.

The truth was, Andy couldn't brush Jerico off. The feelings he had for him were deep-rooted and intense. He couldn't keep stepping around them. He'd have to confront them head on, sooner rather than later.

Chapter Seven

The contractors had done a superb job. Three days after the arson attack and there was no trace of the damage done by the fire. Installation of the bar was complete, the floor had been cleared and prepared ready for the delivery and fitting of the carpets on Saturday, and by the end of the day, work on the kitchen would be complete. The bomb might have come as a shock, but it had done nothing to delay progress on the restaurant.

Jerico bristled with pride as he watched the work come together.

He didn't even need to be here today. He'd spent the morning meeting with the social media team who would spearhead the restaurant's online promotion campaign. His work as executive chef would not begin until Monday, when he'd start training the kitchen staff. Everyone employed to work in the kitchen was an experienced professional. Nothing had been left to chance, and he was certain that by this time next week, they would be ready for the opening night. He could have taken a few hours off this afternoon, but he wanted to be hands on.

It was finally happening. The dream he'd held on to for the last decade was coming to fruition, and he didn't want to miss a moment.

His phone rang, breaking the spell.

"Hi."

"Hello, Jerico. DC Brown here."

Tension coiled inside him as the reality of what had happened early on Tuesday night came crashing back into focus. "Hi. Any news?"

"Well, yes, I'm calling to give you an update. Are you all right to talk?"

"Sure." He stepped away from the workers and out of the back door.

"I'm not sure you'll consider it good news, but you need to be aware."

He stiffened. This did not sound good. "Did you locate Dean Ferguson?"

DC Brown was not going to be hurried. She spoke in a calm, measured fashion. "I talked to the victim liaison officer you told me about and the probation officer who oversaw Mr. Ferguson on licence. What you told me checks out…all of it. The Probation Service supervised him for almost two years. He was released to an address in Durham and eventually got a job there. He was a model offender. He was compliant, never missed an appointment, did all the offence-focused work they asked of him and appeared to display a good understanding of what he had done."

Jerico tutted. It sounded too good to be true. "I feel like there's a 'but' coming soon."

"Your feeling is right. I'm getting there. So, his period of supervision ended last summer, around August. He was still at the same address and holding down the job when they closed his file—a successful completion probation claim."

Jerico was growing impatient. With a deepening sense of gloom, he knew where this was leading. "And?"

"He gave notice on his flat and job last October and hasn't been seen since."

Fuck. "You can't be serious. Eight months and no one knows where he is?"

"He doesn't have any close family. No friends. We're trying to get access to his bank accounts and phone records, but that's not as quick as you might think if you watch any TV crime show. We need to apply to the courts, and that takes time."

"So, he's gone to ground?"

"It very much looks like it."

Jerico leaned against the wall. There was a tightness in chest, like he was in water, out of his depth and the pressure was getting to him. He took a deep breath in through his mouth, trying to get the anxiety under control. "You can save yourself some time and focus your search on Nyemouth."

"We are," she said.

"Then you do think he's here?"

"It would be remiss of us to think anything else. Have you had further incidents? Any malicious messages, criminal damage?"

"No, but if Dean stays true to form, it's only a matter of time."

"Until we manage to locate him, you need to be on alert. If you see him, or even someone who just looks like him, call us. If he's in Nyemouth, he's in breach of the restraining order, and we'll be able to take him in. If we can prove he's responsible for the petrol bomb, we can send him back to prison. Arson with Intent to

Endanger Life is a serious offence. He'll go down for a lot longer than before."

"But in the meantime, he's out there."

"You need to think about your own safety."

Jerico was not worried about that. He'd been boxing since he was fifteen years old. He'd never had to use his fighting skills outside of the ring, but if Dean Ferguson showed his face again, it would be his safety the police should be concerned about. "I'll be all right...just catch him."

As soon as he finished the call, Jerico stamped his foot and smashed his fist into his palm. *Fucking bastard.* Dean's return just as he was about to open the restaurant was no coincidence. He was here to destroy everything Jerico had worked for. *No fucking way.*

Rafiq was on another call when Jerico tracked him down. He waved his hand in his face and gestured for him to wrap it up quickly. Rafiq furrowed his brow. "What?" he mouthed silently.

"Emergency," Jerico whispered.

Rafiq ended the call, and Jerico told him everything. He'd already alerted him to his suspicions about Dean Ferguson and filled him in on their history. The news from DC Brown only cemented what he already feared.

"What do you think he wants?" Rafiq asked.

"To shut us down," Jerico seethed. "In his own twisted mind, he'll think he deserves a place like this, not me. He'll try to destroy it."

"What the hell are we going to do?"

Jerico raked his hands through his hair and groaned. "We'd better get some proper security, twenty-four hours a day until the police catch him. I'm not worried about what he'll do to me. I can take care of that little scrot if he turns up, but I'm concerned about the damage he could do to the property. He'll burn the place to the ground before we even get a chance to open."

Rafiq nodded. "I'll arrange it."

"Okay. I think I'll go home now and print out his photograph. The mug shot from his arrest four years ago is online. He can't have changed all that much. We'll stick copies of it up all over the place, so everyone coming in and out knows who to look for."

"All right but be careful. And try not to worry. They'll find him before next week."

"I'm not worried. I'm furious. The police had better hope they find him before I do."

Jerico's apartment was a fifteen-minute walk from the restaurant. He left his car and set off on foot to give himself a chance to process the news and calm down. He knew he was overreacting. The pressure of the new venue and the upcoming opening was getting to him, but it was more than that. From the moment he had won the *Top Cook* trophy, Dean had been on a mission to taint his success. Ten years of soul erosion had taken a toll. He wouldn't let him take this away.

It was a beautiful late afternoon, and by the time he crossed the river and cut through the back streets towards the residential area, he started to feel calmer. Dean had never bettered him, and he would not allow him to this time, either.

His phone rang again,

Now what? He could handle the current situation but had no resilience left for another drama.

It was Andy. *Thank God.* Finally, someone who could put a smile on his face.

"Hi," he said, and before Andy could get a word in, "you called at just the right time. Can I see you tonight?"

Chapter Eight

The evenings in Nyemouth were beautiful in the summer, when the blue sky was transformed to the most startling shades of purple, pink and red. It was Andy's favourite time of the year, and tonight it was even better, as he walked the South Point cliff with Jerico.

"It reminds me of all those sunsets we saw when we were at sea," Jerico remarked.

Andy nodded his agreement. "I come up here a lot when I have the time, if I get finished at the hotel early enough. It helps me to relax. At this time of year, there's nothing I like more."

"It seems like you've always been drawn to the sea."

"Mmm, probably. I grew up at the coast, worked on ships. I can't imagine ever being far away from it."

He was aware of Jerico watching him and tried to keep his gaze on the path ahead, though the temptation to turn and feast his own eyes was huge. Instead, he filled his lungs with the salty air coming from the water. Up here, the sticky heat of the hotel and the town centre was forgotten.

"What did you do?" Jerico asked. "After we lost touch. You have me at a disadvantage. You can find out about me online, everything I've ever done is there. But you, apart from your professional CV, there's nothing."

Now Andy could not resist looking at him, raising a bemused eyebrow. "So, you've been cyber-stalking me?"

"Doesn't everyone?"

His brown skin looked glorious in the evening light. Andy's mouth was dry. Jerico looked more handsome than he'd ever known him. How had they come to be here, after all this time? Andy knew he wasn't dreaming. This was very real.

He wet his lips. "It's a similar story to your own. I kept working at sea until I was around thirty."

"Doing the same as before? Excursions and tours?"

"For a while, yes. But when I moved to another cruise company, an opportunity arose to join the hotel management side of the ship, and I found I enjoyed that even more. I became Deputy Hotel Manager after just two years. I loved being on the ships. I'm so glad I did all that. For a young guy in his twenties to travel the world and see all those places, how many people are lucky enough to do that?"

Jerico nodded. "It was great, though I don't miss the force-eleven gales and ten-metre waves."

Andy laughed. "Yeah, I think I've pushed those to the back of my mind and just remember the calm waters and sunsets."

"I remember some really bad nights, trying to sing and dance while the stage was going up and down beneath my feet." He gave a dramatic shudder and chuckled.

"But look at it now," Andy said, gesturing to the peaceful North Sea. Tonight, there wasn't even a white cap to ruffle its surface. "When I see it like this, I do miss being out there."

"Would you ever go back? To working on the ships?"

"Nah. Been there, done that. I'm happy here. I've got my dream job and my family close by. I've seen almost all the world has to offer, so now I'm content to stay home. How about you?"

"I've done a couple of themed culinary cruises in the last few years — guest speaking and cookery demonstrations, that kind of thing. It's a lot different on the other side. The guest staterooms are a lot nicer than those tiny crew cabins we had to stay in."

"I'll bet. That's something I've never done, experiencing a cruise ship from a passenger perspective. I imagine it's a different world from what we were used to."

"Yeah, but when you're young, you don't care, do you? You just need a place to sleep and shag. They could have put me in a cupboard, and I'd have been happy." He gave Andy a flirtatious wink.

"I remember what you were like, all right."

They paused and stood side by side and looking out to sea together. For a moment, Andy lost himself in those memories...of standing on the deck of a ship or the shores of exotic countries with Jerico. Were those the best days of his life? No, he decided. The best days were still ahead of him. *Be positive and keep moving forward.*

It had gone eight o'clock. "I'm getting hungry," he said. "Do you fancy something to eat?"

"Starving," Jerico said. "What do you suggest?"

"We could go back to my place." His heart quickened at the suggestion. *What am I doing?* He thought he understood the situation right, but he'd always been bad at reading the moment. "There's barely any wind tonight, and the front garden is sheltered. We could sit outside and have something to eat."

Jerico stepped closer, and he put his arm around Andy's waist. The contact was a sudden and unexpected delight. "Lead the way."

Andy tried to stay cool, but his insides surged like the rough seas they had just been talking about. The warmth of Jerico's hand, the subtle and sexy smell of his aftershave, were doing all kinds of things to him. He couldn't remember the last time a man had made him feel this excited. With Ethan, it had been a fun, friends-with-benefits arrangement, nothing too intense or hot, but Jerico's arm around his waist seemed like the most erotic thing that had happened to him in years.

As they rounded the path that led back towards the houses, Andy was pleased to see the other gardens were empty. Jacob went out most Friday nights, but Matt and Jake often enjoyed a meal outside on a nice evening like this. Andy loved his neighbours, but he didn't want to ruin whatever was developing with Jerico by having to introduce them.

He guided him up the short front path, and as he pulled out his key, Jerico turned to admire the view.

"Holy shit. How on earth did you get this place?"

Andy stopped and joined him, looking down on the River Nye and the town below. From up here, he could see how busy the waterfront was with tourists and visitors. "I was in the right place when it came on the market."

"That's an understatement. You must have snatched the best view in all Nyemouth."

Andy grinned, glad that he liked it. "Actually, that is from the other side." He pointed towards North Point. "The other cliff is a bit higher than this one, and they get some really spectacular views from up there...not that I'm complaining. I love it here."

"I'm not surprised. I thought I was renting a nice apartment, although the view is just of the street opposite, but it's got nothing on this."

"The house is pretty small inside, so don't expect too much." He unlocked the door. "They're about a hundred and fifty years old, and there's not a lot of space for expansion. The yard backs onto the cliff."

Patches came along the hall at the sound of Andy's return. His claws pattering on the wooden floors. He paused, regarding their visitor with curiosity.

"It's okay, Patches." Andy stooped to give the cat a reassuring stroke behind the ears. He raised his head, allowing Andy's fingers to trace the line of his jaw and stroke his chin. "Look at the nice man who's come to see you. He's an old friend."

"Your famous cat," Jerico said. "Will he let me pet him?"

"I'm sure he will. Just give him a minute or two, and he'll come to you. He's a friendly old boy."

"Have you had him long?"

They moved though into the open living room and kitchen space. "He's actually my grandparents' cat. I took him in about seven years ago when they had to go into sheltered accommodation that doesn't allow pets. He's about sixteen now. They rescued him themselves, so no one is quite sure of his age. They think he was a year old at the time but can't be certain."

Aware that he was the subject of their conversation, Patches gave a loud meow, walked a circle around Jerico's legs then brushed his head against him. Jerico squatted to stroke him, and Patches responded appreciatively, giving a satisfied purr. "Wow, he looks great for an older boy." With a broad grin he started talking to the cat and making a fuss over him.

What a lovely sight. His old boyfriend and his cat getting on well together.

Andy went behind the counter and pulled out his stash of takeaway menus. With an award-winning celebrity chef in the house, he wasn't about to resort to his Friday favourite of toasted sandwiches. "Got any preferences?"

"Nah. I've been too busy to check out the competition. I'll defer to your local knowledge. Order whatever you fancy. I will eat anything."

Suddenly, Andy remembered that about him. In their younger days, Jerico had hollow legs when it came to putting food away. He was never full or satisfied. "I'll go with pizza. It will be the quickest and easiest." He phoned in an order for his favourite, a large chicken and mushroom pizza with a cheesy garlic bread and a side order of chips, salad and coleslaw. A ridiculous amount of food for two people, but he had a feeling Jerico would finish it.

He opened a bottle of merlot and put on the outside lights and heater. Patches stuck close to Jerico as they took their seats out front.

"He definitely likes you," Andy said, splashily pouring two glasses of wine.

Jerico continued to make a fuss over Patches. "I think he's just checking me out...to see if I'm good enough for his daddy."

Andy laughed, feeling a heat rise over his face. "You might be right. He's a smart cat."

Jerico glanced at him and held his gaze. The voltage in the gesture sent Andy crashing back to his twenties again. This was all so unexpected. It's like they were picking right up where they had left off fifteen years ago. He wasn't imagining it. The heat and attraction were still there. He didn't know how to process it. He was a grown man, three years off his fortieth birthday, and he felt like a kid when he was around Jerico. Was the feeling mutual? It was too early for Andy to even be comfortable with the answer.

"Have the police made any inroads into your case?" The question was sure to cool the mood, but right now, that's just what he needed.

Jerico grimaced and reached for the wine.

"Sorry," Andy said, "if you don't want to talk about it."

"I'd rather not, if that's okay. It's a long, shitty story, and I don't want to spoil tonight going over it." He sipped the wine. "To tell the truth, I just want to get the damn thing out of my mind, if only for a couple of hours."

Andy winced. *Total fuck up with that question.* "Sorry," he said again.

"You have nothing to be sorry for. I just need to clear my head for a while. Being with you, up here"—he gestured to the view with his glass—"it has helped."

Andy smiled again. "I'm glad for that." He sipped his own wine, then before he knew it, his mouth was running away with him. "I was nervous about this, about being alone with you. Since we met again on Tuesday, I've been kind of… I don't know…mixed up."

Jerico shuffled in his chair, to face him directly. "I'm not mixed up."

"You're not?" His light brown eyes were like tigers in the deepening light. "How come?"

He reached across and put a hand on top of Andy's wrist. The contact sent a heat to Andy's core. "When I opened the door on Tuesday night and saw you, I knew in an instant that I'd been given a second chance. We drifted apart when we were kids, and I'm not saying that wasn't the right thing for us to do at the time. We were so young, we didn't know what we wanted, but I've always regretted that it just..."

"Fizzled out."

"I guess so, yes. I wish I'd tried to keep in touch with you, to stay friends. Who knows what might have happened in another year or two when we knew ourselves a bit better?"

Andy listened, digesting every word. Jerico was giving voice to the exact same thoughts he'd had himself this week.

"Have you had any significant relationships?" Jerico asked. "Ever been married?"

"Nearly...once. About four years ago I came close. My fiancé, Jordan, worked in another hotel. We had a lot in common—friends, interests, work. But Jordan didn't see marriage as reason to give up shagging other guys."

"Shit."

"Yeah, well, better to know that before getting tied down, right? How about you? Has there been anyone significant?"

"Nothing worth mentioning," Jerico said. "A lot of short-term relationships with other hot-headed chefs." He chuckled. "I probably shouldn't tell you this, but chef's make the worst boyfriends."

Andy strove to control the giddiness. "Is that what you're looking for? A boyfriend?"

The tiger eyes stared deep into him. "I didn't think so, not until someone knocked on my door a few days ago. That changed everything."

"Jerico...I don't know what to say."

"Just tell me I'm not wrong to feel this way. That there's a chance you feel the same."

"I do," he said, his heart racing.

Jerico smiled and took his hand. "That's all I needed to know. There's no rush. Hell, it's been fifteen years already. Let's just take things steady and see how it goes. We're different people in different places than we were at twenty-four. I'm looking forward to getting to know you all over again. I don't want to hurry that."

As Andy searched for words, Patches showed he didn't need any. The cat rubbed his head against Jerico's calf and purred appreciatively.

They both laughed.

"I think he agrees with everything you just said."

Chapter Nine

Two men, one middle-aged and podgy, and a younger, slimmer one, both dressed in jeans and matching company polo shirts, erected the sign for Osman's Syrian Kitchen. It had taken them the best part of two hours, using two ladders to carry the circular design and secure it in place, high above the front door.

Dean Ferguson had watched their progress, coming and going throughout the morning, not wanting to draw attention to himself. He had changed his clothes, caps and sunglasses four times, and adopted a different body language whenever he returned to the scene. Dean was a master of camouflage and of going unnoticed—a skill he had learned in prison, when keeping his head down and avoiding attention had become not just a coping mechanism but a method of survival.

He leaned against a low wall on the opposite side of the road. In a baseball cap, baggy shorts, and oversized T-shirt, his small frame allowed him to adopt the guise of a sullen teen. He rounded his shoulders and slouched, mobile phone in a two-handed grip, seemingly fixated on the screen, but behind the cheap sunglasses, his eyes were focused on the men across the street.

The sign they were fixing in place was not what he had expected. He'd thought Jerico would go with something obvious, something large and gaudy with his name written large in coloured lights. Not so. The design was minimal, with the letters constructed effectively from stainless steel. With simple white lights placed behind it, on an evening it would be eye-catching and sophisticated.

Flashy bastard.

Dean' tightened his fingers around the phone, and he drew in slow and steady breaths. Another technique he had learned in prison to minimise conflict risk. His jail mates thrived on confrontation and arguments. They had picked on him mercilessly when he was first admitted, but when their provocations failed to receive a reaction, they had grown bored and left him alone most of the time.

No thanks to Jerico Osman... If it hadn't been for that cunt, Dean would never have been there.

If it weren't for Jerico fucking Osman, Dean would be the one opening his own restaurant now. He'd be the *Top Cook* winner and noted TV personality. And he wouldn't have been launching any Syrian kitchen shit. Dean was a classic cook, serving traditional French and English dishes, none of that Middle East muck.

If it were anyone else, Dean had no doubt that a Syrian-themed restaurant would die on its arse in a town like Nyemouth. The people here were peasants. They wanted fish and steak and pies, not this foreign crap. But Jerico Osman had the luck of the devil. If anyone were going to succeed here, it would be him. He could roll in horse shit and still smell of roses.

Dean's muscles quivered with rage, and heat flushed throughout his body, but anyone looking at him would not see it. If they bothered to glance his way at all, they would see the bored, sullen teen he wanted them to see.

People only ever saw what Dean wanted them to notice.

Jerico Osman had been in Nyemouth for weeks now, and he'd come within touching distance of Dean on at least five occasions. The dumb bastard hadn't recognised him once, hadn't even turned his head to glance. It was hardly a surprise with such a self-centred, self-absorbed prick. Given the hell he'd put Dean through, stealing his championship, taking him to court, allowing him to fester in jail, Dean would have expected some flicker of recognition, but there was none.

From the moment Jerico had cheated and got Dean chucked off *Top Cook*, Dean had meant nothing to him.

That would change soon enough.

At that moment, Jerico and his business partner, Rafiq, came out of the front door. Dean didn't bother to move or try to hide. They wouldn't look his way. They were too caught up in their precious restaurant. They stepped back as far as the pavement would allow, shielded their eyes against the sun with their hands and stared at the sign. A broad, shit-eating grin spread over Jerico's face. Of course it did. What would make a conceited, narcissist happier than to see his own name in massive letters?

The tension in Dean's jaw became painful as he ground his teeth.

Jerico was a vision of happiness. He wore a pair of black trousers, which were obscenely tight on his huge arse, and a white, kitchen tunic. He and Rafiq patted each other on the shoulders, self-congratulatory, like a couple of dumb frat-bros in a film. Jerico gestured with excitement at the sign.

Enjoy it while you can, motherfuckers.

The petrol bomb Dean had thrown on Tuesday night had not been intended to destroy the place. He'd already known the interior was empty, and it would take a lot more than one bottle of petrol to cause much damage, something else he had learned in jail. His intention had been to rattle Jerico, to take the shine off his excitement. Looking at the bastard now, that had only been a fleeting success. The cunt was full of himself again.

But not for long.

Snatches of conversation drifted across the street.

"...great for opening night..."

"...has confirmed and so has *Northeast Living*..."

"...champagne reception..."

Dean's breath sounded loud in his ears. He hoped they choked on the champagne...every fucking one of them. No doubt Jerico had a host of VIPs and influencers lined up to plug his shitty restaurant. Dean hoped the judges of *Top Cook* would be there. He would enjoy wiping the smug smiles from their faces, too. They had been complicit in Jerico's scheme to have him jailed. They've even provided statements to the court on Jerico's behalf, saying Dean had been eliminated because he was the weakest contestant in the heat. They had even lied and said he'd harassed them after the show. If a few letters asking them to reconsider their decision was harassment, then the whole world had gone soft.

Maybe it had...soft enough to think Jerico was a great cook, to put him on TV and spend a fortune to dine at the restaurants he worked for. Dean had visited the one in Newcastle, Palpito, where Jerico had been executive chef. It had cost well over a hundred quid for a piddly tasting menu, another hundred for the matching wines, and it had been disgusting — not even good enough for a dog. And yet they'd had a three-month waiting list for weekend tables.

If people were prepared to pay for that shit then they deserved it.

But Jerico did *not* deserve the acclaim. He was unworthy of the success, of the book deals, the prestige jobs and he was a damn well unworthy of having his own restaurant.

It wasn't right. The bastard was over there right now, admiring the sight of his name, all grand and fancy, about to become the biggest thing in this nowhere seaside town.

Dean couldn't stand it. He'd tried to do something about Jerico once before and had failed. He'd ended up in jail for it. Well, not this time. There would be no mistakes.

Dean was going to take him down. He would ruin his life, destroy his business and by this time next week, he would have annihilated Jerico, too.

Chapter Ten

There was something similar about the backstage area and dressing rooms of most nightclubs. Andy had accompanied his mother to so many gigs over the years that they all tended to merge into one. The glamour he'd known of backstage areas during his cruise days was a world away from these rundown dives. At sea, hygiene was one of the top priorities, but in most shore-based clubs, it barely warranted consideration.

Power Box in Leeds was far from the worst he'd seen. That had been in Chester, where Mari had been performing as part of the celebrations for a drag beauty competition. Panic had broken out backstage when a family of rats had started scurrying around the dressing room. He remembered standing on a table with Mari, screaming, until a fearless drag queen had come in and chased the rats away.

The dressing room at Power Box was tiny, stunk of damp and stale booze, but there was a lingering and reassuring scent of disinfectant beneath it all. Mari sat at a faded mirror and attempted to complete her elaborate stage make-up.

Andy was tired. It was twelve-thirty, and Mari wasn't due on until one. It had been a long day. Nine hours at the hotel, followed by a quick shower and change of clothes, then a two and a half hour drive down the motorway to Leeds. They had stopped at a service station on the way for a late dinner — tough burgers and strong tea — before arriving in Leeds around eleven-thirty. It had taken another twenty minutes of navigating the ring road to find the club.

There was only one chair in the room, and Andy had to lean against the wall behind his mother.

"Go out front and get yourself a drink," she said, looking at him in the mirror as she applied glittering eyeshadow.

"I'm your chaperone, remember? That's what I'm here for."

Mari scoffed. "I think I can manage. Besides, you've already locked my fee away in the car. All anyone can steal from me in here is a few hairpieces and some glitter. Go on. Enjoy yourself. You've got over an hour before we head home. You can watch the show from out front and give me a critique on the drive back. Let me know where I can make improvements."

"You don't need any tips from me. You could play this gig in your sleep."

She rolled her eyes. "And I'd never work again. But I'm serious… Go have a couple of drinks. They will do you good. Besides, I don't want you to see me squeeze my fat arse into my outfit, which is the next step…as soon as I finish my face."

Mari was in great shape, but he wasn't going to waste a breath arguing with her. "Are you changing afterwards?"

"Fuck no. In this place, once is enough. I'll swap my shoes for the drive, but everything will be packed and ready to go the minute I come off stage. Just be back here then."

He gave her a kiss for good luck before heading into the main floor of the club. Nightclubs had never been his thing, even when he was young enough to enjoy them. He'd always been more interested in early morning activities than staying up late to party. He'd been to more nightclubs in his thirties with Mari than he'd ever experienced in his youth.

As he'd expect for Saturday night, the club was crammed to capacity. The crowd was mainly comprised of people under twenty-five, but he was far from the oldest person in there. The heat was unbearable, the atmosphere thick with sweat, perfume and dry ice. It couldn't have been more different from the clear sea air in his beloved garden. It took an age to wriggle through the tightly packed bodies and reach the bar. He ordered a double Jack Daniel's and Diet Coke.

It had been a while since he'd accompanied Mari to one of her gigs. Her boyfriend Richie did most of the honours lately, but it made a change to get out. He would only have spent the night in the house, wondering about Jerico.

He'd done that a lot today. Quay House had been crazy with a wedding in the function room, and the hotel was at full capacity. There had been plenty to keep him busy, but more than once he'd caught himself drifting into a reverie about Jerico. Last night, they had sat outside talking until almost midnight. They'd enjoyed their pizza, and when a chill had cut in, Andy had brought out picnic blankets to keep them warm.

Jerico had been terrific company. Andy was so used to seeing him on TV these days, where he was always the knowledgeable, professional chef, full of great ideas and cooking tips. Behind that, Jerico was as light-hearted and funny as the boy he used to know. At the end of the night, the temptation to ask him to stay had been strong. Andy wanted him. He couldn't fool himself that he didn't, but he held back. The timing hadn't felt right. They had only come back into each other's lives days before. The desire to tear off his clothes and take him to bed was strong, but Andy sensed it would be better if they waited. Better to get to know each other again before adding the complication of sex.

The music at the bar was deafening. It didn't seem to affect the young clubbers who bumped and gyrated, thrusting their bodies together. Andy shuffled to the side of the room, where it was less crowded. He could still see the stage but didn't feel as claustrophobic.

What is Jerico doing now? Asleep? Working late? Preparing for the opening? Andy could pull out his phone right then and find out. He resisted. Almost one o'clock... He didn't want to come across as one of those people who sent lonely messages in the middle of the night.

He sipped his drink and realised he was getting an appraising look from a man several metres away. Not bad looking. Another night, he could have been interested, but not now that Jerico had returned. He made his way nearer to the front, ready for Mari's appearance.

A man in his twenties took to the stage to hype up the crowd. It was crazy how wild they went at the sound of his mother's name. Most of the people in here wouldn't have been born when her songs were on the charts, but it didn't seem to matter. They whooped, hollered and when the intro to her first song began, the screams were deafening.

Mari made her entrance in an emerald-green, full-body catsuit, and the place went wild. She always went down well at these gigs, but he couldn't believe how nuts they were going. Mari had had two massive hits as a featured vocalist for a dance group called The Roman's, followed by three more hits under her own name.

"Let me hear you sing," she shouted to the crowd as she reached the chorus of *Free Your Soul*, a pounding, euphoric house track. The kids in the audience knew every word and belted along with her flawless delivery.

Has she found a new audience? Are her songs big on TikTok or some other social platform?

Andy had seen his mother go down well at countless gigs over the years but never anything like this. As she ran through the set of her five big hits, the place got crazier.

"What the hell happened?" he asked as he got back to her dressing room, as hyped and exhilarated as anyone by what he'd just experienced.

Mari had pulled a white fluffy dressing gown on top of her sequined catsuit and had exchanged her towering heels for flat shoes. Her make-up case and travel bag were closed and ready to go.

"It's been like this all year," she said, swigging from a bottle of water. "I think one of my songs was used in a streaming show last year. Some sci-fi thing or other, I don't know. Never seen it. But I'm getting more gigs than ever, and the crowds are always like this. It's like the bleeding nineties all over again." She gestured for him to take her case. "Come on. Let's get out of Leeds and on the road before we get snarled up in the late-night taxi trade."

Andy carried her things to the car, and by the time he loaded them into the boot, Mari had the engine running and was ready to go.

"Are you sure you're okay to drive?" he asked. "You must be pretty wired after that reception."

She scoffed. "I just want to get home, take this crap off my face and go to bed. I'm looking forward to a long lie-in tomorrow."

"Me, too," he said, unable to stifle a yawn. It was rare to get a Saturday off in the hotel trade, but Andy ensured he took most Sundays and Mondays to recover ahead of another busy week. The motion of the car made him even more tired. He opened a window for fresh air. "I don't know how anyone can bear the heat in those clubs. It was hotter than a sauna."

"It was worse in the nineties. In those days people could also smoke in the clubs. I'd come off stage smelling like I'd performed a show in an ashtray. I could never wear anything twice, even after a short, twenty-minute set."

"Must have been a laugh, though. You wouldn't have done it, otherwise."

"Of course it was. It's the reason I still haul my arse all over the country. I love it. And if they're prepared to pay me, it all tops up my pension pot."

Andy couldn't imagine his mother ever retiring, but it was something she talked about more and more in recent years. At fifty-five, she'd already warned him she would be quitting the hotel at sixty. *"My savings will keep me going until my pension kicks in,"* she had told him after her last birthday.

Despite Mari's concerns about the traffic, they were out of the city in ten minutes and on the motorway home. Now that she didn't have to concentrate on directions, she turned on the radio. A late-night dance station blared the kind of tunes they'd just heard in the club. Mari flipped through the stations in search of something more mellow, before settling on an old ELO record.

"Now *this* is a song," she said, drumming the steering wheel to *Mr. Blue Sky*.

Andy grinned. "Hopefully, we'll have some of those blue skies tomorrow. I don't want to venture any farther than my front garden, and even that won't be until very late morning, if not after lunch. I'm knackered after this week."

"Sorry. I shouldn't have dragged you out tonight. You should be in bed."

"Don't be daft. I'm glad I came. I enjoyed myself. I love to watch you work a crowd like that. There's plenty of time to sleep tomorrow."

He was aware of her looking sideways at him.

"What about Jerico?"

"What about him?" he asked carefully.

"Don't be so bloody evasive. You're not a fourteen-year-old stealing my booze and pretending to know nothing about it. I want to know what's going on. Have you seen him again? *Are* you seeing him again?"

There was no point trying to keep secrets from his mother. She would always sniff out the truth.

"I saw him last night, actually. He came up to the house."

"You *did*. Oh my God, Andy. Why didn't you tell me?"

"Because of this," he said, gesturing to her reaction. "Keep your eyes on the road, please. If you get us killed, there will be no more dates."

"Ah ha. So, it was a date, then?"

He groaned. He'd walked into that one. "I'm not sure. I suppose it was, kind of. It wasn't planned or anything. He sent me a text at the end of the day, and I asked him to come over for a takeaway."

"And?"

"And what? That's it. He came over for a few hours, we had a pizza and he went home."

"Did you shag him?"

"For God's sake, Mam, I don't want to have this conversation with you."

"Why not? I'm not a prude, and you know it. I was hanging out in gay clubs before you were even born. And they were a lot wilder than they are now. There is absolutely nothing that can shock me. So, come on. Did you?"

"No."

"Did he shag you?"

"No," he yelled, unable to stop himself from laughing. "There was no shagging."

She shot him a serious look before returning her eyes to the road. "I sometimes wonder if you're cut out for this gay stuff. You know every other gay I know would have hauled his pants off at the door. I'm damned sure I would have, too."

"Well, I'm not every other gay guy—nor do I want to be. It's...complicated. We've known each before, and it didn't work out. I just need to be sure this time…that we're doing it for the right reasons."

"Son, you can still fuck him and figure out your emotions later. That's what everyone else does."

"I'm not interested in just having sex."

She pricked up at that. "So, what are you interested in? Getting back together? A serious relationship?"

"It wouldn't be the worst thing that could happen," he admitted. "I like him…a lot. I just need to be sure. I'm too old to waste another year or two of my life on someone like Jordan."

"Jordan was a dickhead. You were wasted on him. I tried to tell you that at the time, but you wouldn't listen. I never liked him. Jerico is a million percent better."

"He's also insanely famous and successful. I've never dated anyone like that before. I don't know what his lifestyle involves or whether he'll stay around Nyemouth once his restaurant is established."

"You've got a famous mother, haven't you? And I'm just a regular person like anyone else. Fame only alters people if they allow it to. I don't get that from Jerico."

"You've never met him."

"I've seen him on TV and followed him on Insta. He's sound, I know. I asked Tarot Carole about him, and she agrees."

He scoffed. "I'm not taking advice from your tarot reader. Just give me space to figure out my feelings for myself."

"You just need a little encouragement," she insisted. "I know you said you don't want to waste time on the wrong guy, but you don't want to waste time on nothing, either. It goes too fast. If you like him, follow your heart."

"I do like him."

"Good. Then do something about it."

He groaned. Why had he allowed this conversation to develop? "I already have."

Mari gasped and looked at him hopefully. "And?"

He might as well admit it. She would only nag him for the rest of the journey. "He's coming over tomorrow afternoon, when he gets done at the restaurant."

Her face lit up. "That's more like it, son. Do you want me to cook? I can bring something over."

"Don't you dare. I wish I'd never told you. Just leave us in peace, okay? I want to spend some quiet time with Jerico—just the two of us to figure out where we are in our lives."

"Tarot Carole was right. She told me this would happen."

"Bullshit," he laughed. "And tell Tarot Carole to keep her cards out of my private life."

Despite his protests, Andy was already excited about picking up with Jerico again. Last night they had left off at the perfect place, with both of them wanting more. Tomorrow, he hoped they would take things further, but he would never tell his mother that.

She could get the news from her tarot reader.

Chapter Eleven

Jerico left work at quarter-past-four on Sunday afternoon. He'd hoped to get away by three to spend time with Andy, but the truth was he could have worked through until ten and there still wouldn't have been enough hours in the day. With the opening now less than a week away, time was running at hyper speed. If he hadn't reconnected with Andy, he knew he'd be working nineteen-hours days. Andy was his reason to slow down.

It was another perfect summer day, with blue skies, balmy temperatures and the streets thronged with tourists. Jerico had heard of Nyemouth when he was working in Newcastle, just a forty-minute drive along the motorway, and in the last few years, the town had hit the headlines for all sorts of reasons—murder, violence, scandal, and that was just on land. People seemed to get in trouble every other month and need rescuing from the sea by the fearless lifeboat crew. He hadn't given the town any serious thought, beyond that it didn't sound like the safest of places to live, until he started scouting potential locations for the new business. Rafiq had suggested the seaside town, and on his first visit, Jerico had fallen in love with the place. When he hadn't been working on cruise ships, he'd spent most of his life in cities. He missed the sea, and Nyemouth seemed to offer the best of both worlds, a vibrant town in a beautiful coastal location. He suddenly realised it was everything he'd been looking for.

And that was before he ever knew Andy lived here, too.

He was funky after working in the kitchen all day. Though he was desperate to catch up with Andy, he didn't want to go up there smelling of cooked onions and sweat. He hurried home and took a quick shower before changing into olive green chino shorts and a loose striped T-shirt. The diversion took no more than twenty-five minutes, and he was walking up the bank to Andy's house well before five.

Despite the time of day, the sun was still ferocious, and he was sweating again when he reached the short terrace at the top of the hill. The sound of a radio playing live football came from Andy's garden.

Jerico caught his breath when he reached the gate.

Andy lay on a lounger in the centre of a garden, a large parasol shading him from the intense sun. Jerico hesitated when he realised Andy was asleep. It was a beautiful sight. He wore a pair of short navy trunks and nothing else. He lay on his back, with one arm flung across his face, exposing a small tuft of hair in his armpit. His chest and flat abdomen rose and fell in a gentle rhythm. His long legs were splayed, one straight, the other slightly bent.

His body was lean and muscled, more developed than he'd been in his twenties. He'd had a boyish figure back then, now he was all man.

Jerico flustered at the sight. Andy seemed more attractive every time he saw him.

He hovered by the gate, wondering what to do. He didn't want to barge in and frighten the life out of the poor guy while he slept. At the same time, he was content to wait, to stand there and watch him sleep.

Which is more than a little creepy.

Jerico cleared his throat and said softly, "Andy?" Then he repeated it, just a bit louder.

Andy stirred. The bent leg straightened and the arm across his face fell away. His eyes fluttered open, and he pushed onto his elbows, blinking into focus, looking slightly confused. *And very cute.*

"Hey," Jerico said. "Sorry… I was loath to wake you but felt like a weirdo loitering around your gate watching you."

Andy sat and rubbed both hands across his face. "I didn't know I'd nodded off." He gave a dynamite smile. "Well, don't continue to loiter. What are you waiting for? Come in." There was another empty sun lounger beside Andy's. "I didn't know if you'd want to catch some sun," he said. "What time is it? I left my watch inside."

"Nearly five," Jerico said, admiring Andy's fine figure as got to his feet.

"Shit. I've been asleep almost two hours. Just as well I put the parasol up. I'd be like a boiled lobster by now, otherwise."

Jerico checked him over. "I think you're okay. No signs of burning that I can see. It's my fault. I wanted to be here hours ago."

"Don't worry about it. You're here now. I had a late night, and it's been a tough week. I guess it all caught up with me." He pulled on a white linen shirt. Jerico was pleased when he left it unfastened. "Let's not tempt fate, though. I think I should get into the shade for a while."

The patio area in front of the house was protected from the glare of the sun. Jerico followed him over and took a seat. Andy turned off the football match.

"I'll get us some drinks," he said. "Are you hungry? I've got fresh crab meat, thanks to Jacob next door."

"Not just yet. I'd love a drink, though."

Their eyes locked and lingered for a meaningful moment before Andy smiled and disappeared inside.

Jerico realised his pulse was racing. *I'm not nervous, am I?* No, he reasoned. He was excited and experiencing that strange, old familiar feeling from his youth. When he was with Andy, all his worries about the restaurant, the menus, the opening night, shrank to nothing. He was carefree and happy in a way he wouldn't have believed possible.

A loud meow from the doorway caused him to turn. Patches sauntered out of the house, his tail held high, and brushed against his leg. His soft fur and long whiskers tickled Jerico's bare flesh.

"Hello, handsome," he said, leaning over to stroke him gently from head to tail. The cat gazed up at him with wide, trusting eyes and issued a gentle purr. "You remember me, then." Patches wove around his legs in a figure eight. With his white fur and tortoise-shell patches, it was obvious where he got his name from.

"You've got a little fan there," Andy said, coming out with a bottle of rosé in an ice bucket and two wine glasses. "That's quite a welcome."

"I've never had a cat," Jerico remarked. "I didn't know whether he would like me. We always had dogs when I was growing up."

"Have you never had pets of your own?" Andy set the ice bucket on the table and opened the wine.

"I'm not home enough—long hours, late nights, lots of travelling. I didn't think it would be fair. And I've never had a flatmate or good neighbour I could rely on to look after one while I was out."

"I'm lucky with Jacob next door. He loves Patches as much as I do. Spoils him, really. I feed him cat food, then he goes to Jacob's for fresh prawns and salmon. He's got the best of both worlds."

The cat, seeming to know he was being talked about, moseyed across to Andy and headbutted his leg before letting out an indignant-sounding meow. Andy laughed and stroked his head.

"I know all about your secret ways. Don't try to play innocent with me."

They looked so great together. Andy's adoration for the cat only made Jerico love him more.

Andy poured two generous glasses of wine and passed one to Jerico. "Cheers."

"Cheers." They clinked glasses. "Mmm. Very nice."

"I'm not the biggest fan of rosé," Andy admitted, "but it does go down well on a hot day. Here's to the restaurant. How is it going?"

Jerico shrugged. "Good, I think. I've had openings like this before, but they've always been other people's businesses. I've always been the chef, not the owner. I defer a lot to Rafiq, but it's still a huge amount of extra pressure."

"The reward will be even sweeter in the end," Andy said with enthusiasm. "Because the two of you have done it all together, you'll appreciate it more."

"I hope you're right."

"How far has it come? The venue, I mean, since last Tuesday."

"You wouldn't recognise it. You should come in tomorrow and see for yourself. The bar is all finished and just needs to be stocked. That's happening this week. The decorating is done, carpets fitted. The kitchen is up and running, and I've got staff in now learning the menu. The waiting and bar staff start on Wednesday, ready for the opening on Friday."

Andy relaxed into this chair, stretching out his long, powerful legs. Jerico wondered what he did to stay in shape. He didn't have the obvious build of a gym rat. He was more limber than that...and toned. *Definitely running or walking. Maybe yoga or some kind of resistance work.* His body was truly delicious, with a nice spread of hair across his chest and a tempting treasure trail below his navel.

"It sounds like you've thought of everything. I thought what happened on Tuesday might have set you back, but you seem to have everything in hand."

"It would appear so, but I'm still churned up inside."

"You'll smash it. Bookings must be strong. I was talking to someone yesterday who said they tried to get a table and the first weekend you have available isn't until October."

"Yeah, reservations are great, but bookings can easily be cancelled. If we don't nail the opening weekend and charm the critics, we've had it. We need good press and great word of mouth. If we make it to October, I'll be delighted."

"You're nervous? There's no need to be. You're all anyone is talking about. There's a real buzz out on the place. It's not just because you're a celebrity, either. People are used to having an A-lister like Arnie Walker in town. They are genuinely excited about you and your food."

Jerico shuddered. "Yikes. No pressure, then."

"Everyone is on your side."

"I appreciate it, but it still keeps me up at night. That's why I'm grateful you asked me here this afternoon. It gave me the reason I needed to get away and switch off, if only for a few hours."

"Then we can talk about something else, and you can switch off completely."

"Before we do, I just wanted to let you know that I've reserved a table for the opening on Friday. It's for you and whoever you want to bring."

Andy's mouth opened in surprise. "Are you sure? You must be packed out already."

Jerico grinned. "I'm sure. I'll always find a place for you. I won't be able to see you much. I'll be in the kitchen for most of the night, but it will give me a boost to know you're there. I remember back in the cruise days, I used to perform with greater confidence when you were in the audience."

"You did? You never told me that."

"Sure. Every time."

Andy rolled his eyes. "I can't decide whether you're looking back through rose-tinted glasses, or you're full of BS, but either way, I'll take the compliment."

"It's no bullshit," Jerico said. He couldn't stop smiling. He probably looked like a total goon, but he didn't care. Andy made him happy. It was as simple as that. He sipped the great wine, stretched out his body to absorb the heat and relaxed in the atmosphere. Being here with Andy and Patches was the most chilled he'd felt in months.

Andy turned on his Bluetooth speakers and searched for a playlist on his phone. "Got any requests?"

"I'm easy. Whatever you're into?"

"I'm not very modern in my musical tastes," Andy admitted. "Last night I was in a nightclub in Leeds, and until my mother came on to perform her nineties nostalgia set, the music was dire."

"You go clubbing with your mother?"

"Ha. Not exactly. She was gigging and took me along as her minder." An old nineties dance tune came over the speakers. Jerico recognised it. The Roman's featuring Mari *Free Your Soul*. "This is her."

Jerico sat up straighter. "*What*? Your mum is Mari from The Roman's?"

Andy's eyes sparkled. "Didn't you know?"

"Or course I fucking didn't. Oh, wow, that's amazing." Jerico waved his hands to the euphoric track. "Oh my God, Andy, this is awesome. If she were my mum, I'd be walking around wearing her T-shirts all day, every day."

"Oh, she'd love that. Actually, you should be careful what you wish for. She loves you already. She's a big fan of yours."

"She is? I hope you'll bring her on Friday, then?"

"Are you kidding? Once she finds out you've set aside a table, there'll be no way of stopping her. Try keeping her away."

The late afternoon passed in a pleasurable whirl. They finished the rosé, laughing and reminiscing as they listened to a roster of old-school dance bangers. They moved over to the sun loungers. Jerico took off his T-shirt and laid back, soaking up the heat. He was pleased to catch Andy checking him out as he stripped. He'd been so busy with work that he'd neglected his regular gym and boxing routines these last two weeks, but his body was holding up okay. In another week or so, he'd try to get back to his boxing classes and return his physique to prime condition. Jerico didn't work out to look good. It was more important to feel good, but with a hottie like Andy in his life, it wouldn't hurt to look as good as he could.

"I'm starting to feel a bit tipsy," Andy admitted when all the wine was gone.

"Have you eaten today?"

He stretched his arms above his head and arched his strong back, giving it some thought. "Erm...no, not since breakfast. I'd better have something before I get too drunk. Besides, Patches will want his tea any time now."

"So, what are you cooking up with this crab?"

Andy sat up. "Oh, I'll leave the cooking to you, if you don't mind. I'm not about to embarrass myself in front of a top chef. We're having crab salad with potatoes and sourdough bread."

"Sounds delicious," Jerico said. "The most beautiful food is always the simplest. And fresh crab shouldn't be spoiled."

"I have a confession to make. I didn't cook the crab, either. Jacob did the honours and brought it around already prepared at lunchtime. I am going to chop the stuff for the salad, if that counts." He got to his feet.

Jerico rose with him. "Mind if I come in with you? I'm good at chopping, too."

Was that a hint of colour in Andy's cheeks? "I'd love that. Follow me."

Jerico was glad that Andy left his shirt on the lounger and walked towards the house bare chested.

"Hey, you got a tattoo," he said, noticing the dragon design on Andy's shoulder. He moved in for a closer look.

Andy groaned. "Oh, don't remind me. It's out of sight, so I prefer to forget about it."

"Don't you like it?" The design wasn't great. The edges were blurred, and the colours had faded to a murky green.

"I *hate* it. It's the result of a drunken stayover in Gran Canaria many years ago. Three of us from the crew thought it was a cool idea at the time. It wasn't the prettiest tattoo in the first place, and now it looks fucking hideous. I'd get it removed if I didn't have far better things to spend my money on. Thank God I didn't get it anywhere more visible. Besides, I leave it there as a reminder never to do anything so stupid again."

Jerico chuckled and let his eyes fall to something far more appealing as they went into the house — Andy's arse. He'd always had a cute little butt, but like the rest of him, it had filled out with age into something bigger, broader and a whole lot sexier.

As they went into the kitchen, they were accompanied by the eager ting-a-ling of Patches' bell as he trotted in behind them. He meowed excitedly and danced around Andy's feet.

"I can see who's in charge around here," Jerico said.

"Oh, yeah. He's definitely the boss of me. I know my place." He opened a sachet of cat food and spooned it into a bowl, all the while Patches grew louder and more insistent until Andy put the bowl down for him. Then the only sound he made was the eager lapping of gravy.

"Wow," Jerico said, watching the cat attack the food without pause.

"Yep. For an old boy, he's lost none of his appetite. If anything, he wants even more food than he used to. Now that he's satisfied, we can get on with our own dinner." He opened the fridge door and started taking out salad ingredients.

"I'm not that hungry yet," Jerico said, stepping closer. He could resist no longer. Andy's body had been driving him crazy the whole time. "For food, that is."

Andy stopped what he was doing. A knowing smile hovered over his lips, and he turned to face Jerico.

Was that a thickening hardness he could detect in the front of his trunks?

Jerico moved towards him and slid a hand onto Andy's waist. He'd been longing to touch him all week. Then their chests and bellies were pressing, and their lips touched. Jerico wrapped his other hand around Andy's head, pulling him in to deepen the kiss. They moved their tongues against each other, and the hardness in Andy's groin matched his own.

At last, they broke apart, grinning.

"That was worth waiting for," Jerico murmured, their foreheads touching.

"It was," Andy said breathlessly. "And so is this."

Without another word, he took Jerico's hand and led him to the stairs.

Chapter Twelve

Andy bounded up the stairs ahead of Jerico, brimming with excitement. He'd had a hopeful feeling this is where the afternoon might end and had gone to the effort of changing the bed that morning and opening the windows wide to air out the room. As they entered, he went straight over and closed them again. He knew how well the sound travelled up here on South Bank and didn't want to broadcast what they were doing to the whole terrace.

"Very nice," Jerico said, coming in behind him.

"Yes," Andy agreed. "My bedroom has one of the best views in town."

"I'm not talking about *that* view." Jerico moved in behind him, putting his hands on Andy's waist and pressing his chest into his back. "I mean *you*."

His breath was hot on Andy's neck, and when he touched his lips to it, Andy shuddered, goosebumps rippling down his spine. Jerico followed the line of his neck, nuzzled into his ear. Andy gasped. He revelled in the attention and leaned into him, planting his arse against his groin, feeling the heat and unmistakable hardness. He rolled his hips in small circles, getting a good impression of his dick. Jerico was one of the girthiest guys he'd ever known. He remembered that much about him.

"This feels good," Jerico crooned in his ear.

Andy raised his head to the ceiling, surrendering further as Jerico slid his hands across his abdomen, causing him to shudder again. They moved upwards until his fingers found his nipples. He grazed them with the gentlest touch before taking hold of the tips and squeezing.

Andy murmured appreciatively.

"See?" Jerico said. "I remember how much you like that."

"What else do you remember?"

"About you? I remember everything. But my memory is not what it used to be. How about a refresher course?"

Andy chuckled.

Jerico's hands were back on his waist. He tucked his fingers into Andy's swimming trunks and eased them down. Andy didn't resist. He closed his legs to let the trunks slide down and kicked them away. He was completely naked while Jerico still wore his shorts and sneakers, and it felt wonderful — liberating and sexy as hell.

Jerico buried his face in Andy's neck while his hands went to his groin. He groaned enthusiastically when he wrapped one hand around the shaft of Andy's cock and cupped his balls with the other. Andy gasped, and his cock swelled harder than he could remember in years — a real young man's hard-on. Jerico trailed his fingers along the underside until he reached the head. He gently tugged and stretched Andy's foreskin.

"It's just like I remembered," Jerico whispered. "Only better."

"You have me at a disadvantage. You're still wearing clothes."

"Let me enjoy you a little bit more."

Andy turned, wrapping his arms around him to savour another deep, soul kiss. Jerico's hands went straight to his bare buttocks, taking each cheek in a firm grip.

"You've filled out in the most magnificent way," Jerico said, between kisses.

There were a lot of things Andy didn't like about getting older, but beefing up in the body wasn't one of them. He'd found it near impossible to bulk up in his younger days and had been skinny as hell until his late twenties. He liked his slightly chunkier, more mature body, and from the way Jerico handled his arse, he must like it too.

Jerico kneaded his butt as they kissed. He spread Andy open, allowing the cooler air of the room to caress his hot crack. Andy ground his hard cock against Jerico's hips.

"We really need to even the score here. Get those pants down."

Jerico grinned and fumbled with his belt, unfastening his shorts.

Jerico's body had also changed with the years. He was more muscular than before, beefier all over. His chest and belly were hairier, too. It all made Andy appreciate just how young they had been the first time around, little more than boys. Now they were men with the weight and strength to prove it.

Jerico's shorts dropped to the floor, and he stepped out of them. He wore a pristine pair of white briefs underneath. He was about to shuck them down when Andy grabbed his wrists to halt him.

"This is my treat," Andy murmured.

Jerico beamed. "I'm all yours."

Andy lingered over his hips, tracing his fingers along the waistband of those tighty whities, sifting through the dark curls that coated Jerico's abdomen. Jerico twitched and shivered.

"It tickles," he gasped.

Andy planted both hands on his waist before moving them back to explore the generous curves of his arse. *Oh, yeah, prime daddy arse.* Jerico's buttocks were huge, and he cupped them in his palms, feeling their weight, their firmness. He slipped inside his briefs, feeling the heat of skin against skin. His butt was furry. Andy appreciated the soft hair beneath his fingers.

He dropped to his knees, his hands still planted on Jerico's arse, and moved his face closer to his crotch, inhaling the scent of him, feeling the heat that radiated from his groin. Jerico's fat cock strained against the white cotton. The outline was thick. Andy remembered how big he was. He hadn't had a lot of experience when they were first together, and it had been a challenge to take Jerico's big dick the first few times they'd fucked. Would it be any easier now? Probably not. Andy had become more of a top in the last few years. He was out of practice.

"Do you still…?" He searched for the words, unsure how best to frame the question. "Er, are you still a top?"

Jerico gave a gentle huff of mirth. "I'm a lot more relaxed than I used to be, if that's what you mean. I don't always have to do the fucking. Sometimes I don't do it at all. Fucking isn't everything. There are plenty of other things we can do if it bothers you. But I'm versatile these days, if you do want to, that is."

Now Andy laughed. "I was just wondering." He took his hands off Jerico's arse and stroked his cock through his briefs. "This is pretty intimidating when I haven't had anything inside me for a while."

Jerico leaned into his hand. "I'm cool with anything you want to do. You set the pace."

"Oh, I want you all right. I want *all* of you."

He pulled Jerico's briefs down, eyeing his huge cock as he stepped out of his underwear and kicked them away. *Jesus, it's even bigger than I realised.*

Andy knew he would have to take baby steps to work himself up to this thing. He started with the head, taking it into his mouth and sucking gently. Soon his tongue was tingling with the old, familiar taste of Jerico's pre-cum. He took his generous nuts in his hand, remembering how Jerico used to like having them squeezed during sex. He juggled them in his palm while sucking. Jerico's appreciative groans let him know he was doing everything right.

In all these years, Andy had never believed he might find himself doing this again, being down on his knees, servicing this man and revelling in how good it was to have him in his mouth again.

"Easy," Jerico said. "That's far too intense. Much more and I'll be finished."

Andy steadied himself on Jerico's body and got to his feet. Their cocks bounced together as they came in for an embrace, locking their mouths, tongues duelling in a kiss.

"This is crazy," Andy said, "in a good way. Like déjà vu, but not the same, either."

"I think I know what you mean. And I'm not complaining. Quite the opposite."

Andy took his hand and led Jerico to the bed. They fell on it together and resumed their kissing. Jerico rolled on top, pressing him into the mattress with his weight. Andy stretched and luxuriated beneath him, opening his thighs, wrapping his arms around him. He wanted to savour all of him, every second of this experience — with his hands, his skin, his eyes, his nose. The scent of Jerico's body drove him crazy. Andy shoved his nose into Jerico's hair and inhaled deeply.

They rolled over, and now Andy was on top, pushing his trunk against Jerico's. Jerico's hands were in the small of his back, sending shivers of pleasure all along his spine. They gasped and writhed and explored each other.

"You're beautiful," Jerico whispered. "You always were, only now you're even better, if that's possible. You're gorgeous."

Andy answered him with a kiss. He'd never been good at taking compliments and didn't know how to reply without sounding corny. The easiest way was to show Jerico just how attractive he found him. He wondered why he'd been wasting his time fooling around with a boy like Ethan, when what he'd needed all along was a man. But if he hadn't kept things on a casual basis with Ethan, he might not have been available when Jerico returned to his life. That didn't bear thinking about.

Jerico opened his legs and wrapped them around Andy's waist, angling his hips upwards until Andy's cock nestled in the crack of his arse. He took Andy's head in both hands and looked straight at him, his brown eyes sparkling with desire.

"I want *you* to fuck me," he said.

Arousal surged through Andy. He remembered fucking Jerico back in the day, but it hadn't been often. Jerico had always seemed uncomfortable with the act, as though he couldn't wait for Andy to be finished and get it over with.

"Are you sure?"

He nodded. "Absolutely. I want it. I want *you*. I want to show you I've changed for the better."

Andy leaned down to kiss him again before crawling to the edge of the bed. There was a box of latex-free condoms in the bedside drawer and a bottle of lube. He retrieved both. "Which way will be easiest for you?"

Jerico grinned. "Better take me from behind. I come fast when I'm on my back. Don't want to peak too soon." He rolled over and got onto all fours, presenting his delicious, meaty rump.

"So, you've become more versatile?" Andy took a condom from its wrapper and rolled it down his cock.

"I'm probably still sixty percent top, forty bottom. It depends on my mood." Looking over his shoulder, he added, "And the man I'm with."

Andy stroked his arse. He'd been right about the hair. Jerico's checks were covered in a fine layer of dark, silky hair. The sight of it made him even harder. "I'd say I'm fifty-fifty. I like it either way. Like you, it depends on the guy." He gave Jerico's beefy butt a playful slap. "But an arse like this is too hot for me to resist."

He drizzled lube into Jerico's butt crack then got to work with his fingers, massaging the hole before easing inside. He was tight—very—but Andy entered him with his finger easily, preparing the way.

"Is that all right?" he asked, pausing so Jerico's body could adjust.

"You'd know if it wasn't." Jerico gently wiggled his arse. "I won't break. Get inside me."

Andy palmed more of the lube and coated his cock from tip to root. He didn't want to take any chances and hurt the gorgeous man beneath him. He got in position behind him, guided his cock into position, nudging the opening. He put one hand on Jerico's hip and pushed slowly past the resistance, entering his hot depths. "Oh, God," he sighed, as Jerico's arse gripped him.

"Yeah," Jerico groaned encouragingly. "Fill me up. Remind me of what I've been missing."

Andy pushed deeper, deeper, until his hips pressed against Jerico's chunky buttocks. He was all the way in. He took Jerico's hips in both hands and held the position, letting his cock sit inside him, teasing him with a slowly deliberate pulse.

"Oh, man," Jerico moaned with delight. "That's fucking intense."

"Tell me when you're ready."

"For you? I've been ready for the last fifteen years. I just didn't know it. Fuck me to make up for the lost time."

Encouraged, Andy withdrew before taking up a long, slow stroke, tantalising Jerico's hole with every inch of his cock. He wanted to give him maximum pleasure.

Jerico dropped his head and shoulders to the bed, surrendering entirely. He sighed and moaned with every thrust. Soon, his brown skin glistened with sweat. It had never been like this before. Andy had never seen him take such delight in getting fucked. Jerico had changed in more ways than he could have imagined. Andy had to control his own pleasure. This moment was so intense he was on a hair trigger, and he wanted it to last as long as possible.

They gradually changed position, Jerico rolled onto his side, and hooked his elbow around the back of his leg, raising it to give Andy unrestricted access. Now Andy could see pleasure written across Jerico's face as he gave it to him. Jerico's brow furrowed, his eyes were closed, and he breathed heavily through his mouth. His face was flushed and slick with sweat. Eventually Andy rolled him onto his back. This was the best. He looked at Jerico and kissed him. They breathed heavily into each other as they fucked.

"I…can't…hold…for long," Jerico said. Andy loved the helpless catch in his voice.

"I'm close, too. Ready when you are."

Jerico nodded. His breath quickened into a hiss, and he bit his bottom lip. He came without touching his cock, letting out a desperate cry as he propelled a massive spurt of spunk across his belly — then another, and another. His hole tightened as he came, and that was all it took to pull Andy over the edge of orgasm with him. Andy gripped his body tight as he came in great, shuddering waves.

"Holy shit," Jerico yelled when the pleasure subsided. "That was incredible."

Andy lay on top of him, bearing his weight on his elbows. He buried his face against Jerico's neck and laughed. "You're not kidding." He sucked in great lungfuls of air. "Oh my God."

"Totally." Jerico held on to him, with his legs wrapped around Andy's waist, keeping him in place. "But if you think that makes up for the time we've lost, you're wrong. We've got a lot of catch-up sex to have."

They both laughed, utterly content and lost in each other.

* * * *

They were fucking. They had to be. Jerico had been in there too long for anything else. Dean had seen the way they'd looked at each other when they were out in the garden—too turned on to even know he was there. *Dirty bastards.*

Dean had followed Jerico all the way from work to his flat, then to this house and the guy he'd hooked up with earlier in the week. Jerico hadn't even noticed he was there. Dean was pleased with himself. He'd become a master of disguise. The dumb fucker who had taken out a restraining order against him had no idea that Dean had been no more than five metres away from him several times today.

The guy he was fucking worked at Quay House. *Might even be the manager.* Dean had seen him a couple of times when he'd been working casually at The Lobster Pot. Andy something or other was friends with the manager and had been in for food a couple of times while he was there. He'd thought he would have had better taste than to fuck a low-life like Jerico.

He'd wandered past the house a few times while they'd been sitting in the garden, changing his cap or his T-shirt from the supply he kept in his backpack, adjusting his posture to appear like someone else. They'd been too caught up in each other to take any notice of what was happening beyond the garden gate.

Even now, while they were inside screwing, they'd left the front door of the house wide open. A scruffy old cat was sunning itself on the lawn, but otherwise, the place was unattended. Dean could walk right in, and they wouldn't have a clue until he pounced. He'd been tempted, too. It would have been easy, and the looks on their faces when he caught them in the act would have been priceless.

But he'd resisted. Tonight was not the time to reveal himself. There was so much more damage he wanted to do to Jerico Osman, so many ways to torment him.

And now, he'd been granted a whole new set of opportunities. His plan of attack had always been via the restaurant, but now Jerico had formed an emotional attachment to the hotel manager, so many more ways to hurt him presented themselves.

With a crooked smile, Dean turned away from the house and headed down the bank. He had planning to do, and if it kept him up all night, he would enjoy every moment of it.

Chapter Thirteen

Andy lay on his side, watching Jerico as he slept. It had been a night of unending pleasure, and neither of them had gotten much rest. Their appetite and hunger had rivalled anything from their younger days. If anything, the energy between them was stronger now than it had ever been. Despite so little sleep, Andy had never felt more awake or invigorated.

If anyone had asked him a week ago if this was what he wanted, he would have scoffed at the idea. Jerico Osman was a figure from the past who had no place in his present life. Of course, he'd been aware of Jerico's business in Nyemouth—there couldn't be a person in the town who wasn't—but he'd always thought that when they met each other again, it would be as friends. Too many years and differing experiences had passed for there to be any romantic connection. They weren't young men anymore, excited to be travelling and seeing the world—and for a few brief months doing it together. They were adults, at different places in life, with their own careers and commitments.

Jerico's fame didn't intimidate him. He was used to it with his mother. Even now, when working in the hotel, she got recognised, and fans of her music would often arrive at reception with CDs and twelve-inch records for her to sign. Jerico's celebrity didn't bother him at all. It just seemed to Andy that they had had their moment fifteen years before, and it would be foolish to think they could ever experience it again.

But here they were, having done exactly that — one night of wild, abandoned passion.

And it was better than before. With the experience they'd gained in the years apart, they'd been able to satisfy each other in ways he had never anticipated.

Now what? Where did they go from here? Was this it? Had they scratched an itch and could go their separate ways again? That was the last thing he wanted. And Jerico had offered him a table at the opening night of the restaurant. Didn't that suggest he wanted more than a one-night stand, too.

Stop overthinking. Just enjoy the moment.

Jerico stirred beside him and opened his eyes. He saw Andy looking at him and grinned. "How long have you been awake?"

"Not long. Patches is calling for his breakfast. I'll have to go down and feed him in a minute before he starts scratching at the door."

Jerico flung an arm over his waist. "Give me a couple of more minutes before Patches takes you away from me."

Andy loved his goofiness. That was one part of him that hadn't changed. "Don't you have to go to work?"

He groaned. "I suppose so. How about you?"

"No, day off."

"All right for some. What time is it, anyway?"

"Just gone eight."

Jerico sighed, stretched and rolled onto his back. "Ugh. No rest for the wicked."

"This time next week when Osman's is open to paying customers, it will all be worth it."

"Ha. Let's just get to Friday first. No, scratch that. Let's just get through today."

"You're worrying about nothing. After everything else you've achieved, you should have faith in yourself now."

"I do," he said, staring at the ceiling. "But that doesn't keep me from worrying. And the bastard who threw the petrol bomb the other night is still out there. Fuck knows what else he's got in mind."

Andy rose onto an elbow. "Do you really think he will? It could have been random, a one-off attack. Nyemouth is a nice place, but there are plenty of fucked up people here. If you don't believe me, Google some of the headlines from the last few years for a summary of our greatest hits."

Jerico screwed up his face. "Oh, now you tell me I've moved to looney town."

Andy laughed and tickled his belly. "Maybe you should have done your research before making such a big investment."

"I knew about the Arnie Walker thing and some of the other stuff, but I'll spare myself the details of the town's other horrors until after we open."

Andy got out of bed and pulled on a pair of loose shorts. "Have you got time for a quick breakfast before you go?"

Jerico nodded, rolling off the bed and searching for his clothes.

"Oh, hang on," Andy said. "I've got bacon. Do you eat that?"

"Don't worry. I'm one-hundred-percent agnostic. I'll eat anything you put in front of me."

Andy headed downstairs while Jerico went to the bathroom. Patches waited impatiently in the kitchen and meowed loudly.

"Calm yourself. It's coming now."

He put down a bowl of cat biscuits and a fresh bowl of water before taking Patches' litter tray out to the bin, returning with a fresh one. He scrubbed his hands then put the kettle on and set about making breakfast. The bacon was sizzling in the pan when Jerico came down.

"Smells good," he said, sliding into a seat at the kitchen table.

Andy poured two glasses of orange juice. "How do you like it? Crispy?"

"Fairly well done is good."

Andy threw some chopped mushrooms into another pan and sliced open two large bread buns.

"I owe you a meal," Jerico said. "You feed me every time I come here."

"I'm coming to your place on Friday night, aren't I?"

"Today is Monday. Do you think I want to wait that long? What are you doing tonight?"

Andy kept his cool, though inside he was ecstatic. His fears that Jerico was only looking for a fuck for old times' sake were unfounded. "No plans."

"Great. Is eight o'clock too late for you? I doubt I'll finish work before seven."

"Eight is fine. I always eat late."

"Excellent. How about that place in the marina, The Lobster Pot? My treat."

"Oh, no. That's really expensive. All I've given you is a takeaway, a salad and one breakfast."

"Don't worry about the cost. Besides, it'll give me a chance to check out the competition. I'll book a table for eight. Are you okay just to meet me there?"

Andy laughed. "It's less than a ten-minute walk from here. I'm sure I'll make it."

"Then it's a date…a proper one."

Andy served up the bacon and mushroom sandwiches. Jerico smothered his in tomato ketchup and took a huge bite.

"Mmm," he said through a full mouth.

He devoured the sandwich before Andy had eaten a third of his own.

"There's more bacon in the fridge, if you want another one." He'd forgotten what a big appetite Jerico had.

He wiped his mouth and stood. "It was beautiful, but I've got to get going. I want to rush home for a shower and change of clothes before going into work." He leaned in and kissed him on the cheek. "Thanks for a wonderful night and a beautiful breakfast. I'll text you when I get confirmation of the restaurant booking, and I'll see you there at eight."

Andy appreciated one last look at his mighty arse as Jerico crossed the room and let himself out.

Wow. Pinch me.

Patches jumped onto Jerico's empty seat and gazed at Andy with smiling eyes.

"So, what do we think? Does he get your approval?"

Patches gave a low meow that Andy took for yes.

"I'm glad you like him, too," he said.

He finished his sandwich, before making a cup of tea and carrying it out into the front garden. It was another warm, cloudless morning, more akin to the Mediterranean than the northeast coast of England. At least he wouldn't have to spend the day sweltering in a suit in a hot office. The sun had yet to reach the front of the house, so he dragged a chair to the bottom of the garden where he could get some rays.

"Morning," a cheery voice called.

He hadn't spotted Jacob on the other side of the fence, enjoying a coffee in his own garden.

"Morning, Jacob, beautiful day." He went over to the fence so he wouldn't have to shout. "Thanks again for the crab. It was gorgeous. We had it with salad and potatoes last night."

"I'm glad you enjoyed it. I've got a little of the brown meat left. I only like the white part myself but wondered if Patches would fancy finishing it off for lunch."

"I think you'll have a very happy cat on your hands if you give him a little of that."

"I'll save it for when he calls in later." Jacob sipped his tea and said, "I saw your friend on his way a few minutes ago."

Andy laughed. "Nothing gets past you."

"I take it you managed to rekindle the old flame, then?" His bright blue eyes were hopeful.

A warmth flushed Andy's face. "I suppose that's what you could call it. Yeah, we did."

"That's great. I'm so pleased for you. He seems like a nice fella. I sometimes wonder when I see people on TV whether it's all an act, but he seems entirely genuine. I have a pretty good sense of when people are putting it on, and I have a good feeling about him."

"I do, too, but I'm going to take my time. I don't want to rush things when he's got so much going on with his restaurant. He's going to be crazy busy once he opens next week."

"Everyone is busy," Jacob said. "That's no reason to deny yourself some personal happiness. I'm telling you…life isn't forever, and the days only get shorter as you get older. Don't take things too slowly, otherwise you might regret wasting the time when you had it."

* * * *

Andy spent a lazy morning around the house dealing with the mundane weekly chores. He had a housekeeper who came one afternoon a week to take care of the basic cleaning and to iron his laundry, but each Monday he liked to vacuum the house from top to bottom to keep on top of the cat hair, change his bed and clean the bathroom. Usually they were necessary but boring jobs, but today he breezed through the tasks, stopping now and then to dance along with the Steps greatest hits playlist he'd put on. *Perfect housework music.*

He took a long shower and washed his hair before putting on clean shorts and a T-shirt. He'd have to change into something smarter for their date this evening, but for now, comfort and coolness were the priorities. He made a salad from the leftovers he had from yesterday and opened a can of tuna, which he had to share with Patches. Seafood was the cat's greatest passion, and there was no way Andy could ever enjoy tuna, prawns or salmon without giving Patches his share on a saucer.

As he was loading the dishwasher, his phone pinged with a text alert. *Jerico.*

Table booked for eight. How about meeting at seven-forty-five for a quick cocktail before the meal?

Andy replied that he'd be there. Jerico had done well to get a table on such short notice at the height of the season. He wondered whether his high profile had helped to secure the booking. Though he was about to open a rival business, the appearance of such a well-known chef would also be good publicity for The Lobster Pot.

There were a few things Andy needed from town. After lunch, he locked up the house and headed down the bank. As he was leaving, Patches leapt over the fence into Jacob's garden, no doubt looking for more treats. He'd be in for a real surprise when Jacob dished up a saucer of crab meat. Andy knew that both he and Jacob spoiled the cat, but he no longer cared. Patches was a wonderful companion, and at sixteen, he was the equivalent of being in his mid-to-late seventies in human years. The old boy deserved a good life in his later years.

The early afternoon heat caught Andy by surprise. He was halfway down the hill when he realised he'd forgotten to pick up his sunglasses and cap to protect him from the sun. He stuck to the shaded side of the street most of the way down, but once he reached the marina, there was no shelter.

Yikes. The heat is fierce.

Once he'd done what he needed at the shops, he would call in to The Seagull Café for a coffee and some shelter before making the trek back home.

His thoughts were so caught up in what he had to do and of seeing Jerico later that he failed to notice the man on a bike riding towards him. He only looked up as he thought the man was about to ride into him.

He wore a baseball cap, sunglasses and a medical face mask.

It took less than a second to realise this must be the man who had started the fire at Jerico's on Tuesday night.

The man's hand jerked towards Andy, and a second later he felt cold liquid hit him full in the face.

He had only one thought. *Acid attack.*

Andy had barely recovered from the shock when his eyes began to burn.

Chapter Fourteen

The kitchen staff presented a selection of the dishes from the menu Jerico had asked them to prepare. He worked his way along the line, checking the appearance of each sample.

"Try to keep it more central," he said to Ismal, one of the new chefs. The food was all on one side of the plate with a lot of empty space. "And it needs more sauce. It's meant to be tasted, not just for show."

"Yes, Chef," Ismal said, deadly serious.

Jerico dug his fork in, picking up a good amount of lamb, couscous and sauce, and tasted all in one. He chewed slowly, considering the flavour and texture. "Wonderful," he said. "The meat is so well cooked it's just falling apart, and your spices are perfectly layered. That's exactly how I want it to be for every portion, every serving. Well done."

"Thank you, Chef."

Jerico was delighted with the performance from all his new team. There were a few minor things to be refined, but overall, he'd chosen a talented and enthusiastic bunch, and the early indications were that they worked well together. The proof would come next weekend when they had to work under the time pressure of serving real customers rather than the test plates he required of them now, but he was confident in their abilities.

He worked his way along the counter, giving comments and feedback in minute detail. He wasn't one of those chefs who got off on belittling his staff, screaming and swearing during service. Quiet conviction was more effective, and he believed in giving praise where it was due, but he knew what he wanted and was exacting at ensuring he got it.

"Great work, everyone. Okay, fifteen minutes till your next plate. Go."

The team hurried back to their workstations to practice their next dishes.

Jerico was feeling remarkably calm. The nerves were bound to kick in later in the week, closer to opening, but for now, he was relaxed and confident. He was sure he owed as much of that to Andy than anything that was happening here in the kitchen. Last night had left him in the best mood ever. It had been a struggle to keep the smile from his face all day. Every time his thoughts returned to Andy, he got the greatest, fuzzy warm feeling inside.

What a night it had been. The sex had been insanely hot, not that sex was what mattered. They had reconnected in a spiritual way he hadn't thought possible. Jerico believed in fate, and if Andy had come back into his life right now, there had to be a reason for it. It was meant to be.

There were loud voices from the front of the restaurant. He couldn't make out what was being said but recognised the urgency of the tone.

Oh, here we go. Now the wheels are about to fall off the bus.

He went through to the dining room. A couple of men were fixing artwork to the walls. Rafiq was at the front door talking to a man he did not recognise, who wore a pair of chef's trousers and an apron. Rafiq turned as Jerico approached and he instantly clocked the worry on his face.

"What's up?"

"There's been an incident," Rafiq said.

The man at the door stepped forward. He was in his late twenties, early thirties and very good-looking. "Hi. I'm Jake. I'm a neighbour of Andy's. I own the café in the marina. Andy's there now, and he asked me to fetch you." The young man's expression was deadly serious, and the tone of his voice was grave.

Fuck. Something has happened.

"Is he all right?"

Jake gave an uncertain nod. "It's best if you just come with me, and I'll explain on the way."

Jerico hurried forward. "Come on, then. What the hell is it? What's happened?" His mind was already turning to Dean Ferguson. What had he done now? The petrol bomb the other night hadn't been enough for the bastard. He'd had to escalate things and hurt Andy.

They walked quickly down the street, elbowing their way through the crowd.

"Someone rode up when he was walking through town and threw something in his face."

An anxious bird took flight in Jerico's chest. "Shit. What was it?"

"We thought the worst at first…that maybe it was acid," Jake said.

The anxiety was replaced by nausea. "Oh my God," he gasped. "Andy."

"It's okay," Jake continued. "A couple of customers witnessed the whole thing and brought him straight in. We poured litres of water over his face. But it can't have been acid, because his skin is okay. There's no inflammation. No damage. No burning. I think he'll be all right."

"Oh, thank God." Jerico's fear did not subside.

"We wondered if it was just a prank, someone trying to scare him by throwing water, but he complained that his eyes were stinging. And there was a smell. It must have been alcohol. Cheap vodka or something like that."

"Is he okay?"

"I think so. My sister and some customers were administering first aid when he sent me to find you. We've got eye-wash kits in our first aid box. A customer rang the NHS helpline, and they've done everything they advised…flushing out as much of the alcohol as possible."

"Who the fuck did it? Did they see who it was? These witnesses."

"Just that it was a man on a bicycle, wearing a face mask and dark glasses. He rode up to Andy and emptied a bottle in his face before taking off. It was all over before they had a chance to react or stop him. I think they were more concerned about getting help than catching the prick who did it."

Dean. There was no doubt about it now. *The motherfucker. Why haven't the police caught him yet?*

They reached the marina. A crowd gathered on the street in front of The Seagull Café. Jake barged straight through, gripping Jerico's arm and dragging him in his wake. He wondered why there wasn't an ambulance there. Even if Dean had used vodka rather than acid, surely Andy required medical treatment to avoid permanent damage to his eyes.

The interior of the café had been cleared of customers. Andy sat on a chair towards the rear with three people standing over him. He had his head tipped back and held his lids open while a young black woman poured water into his eyes. He winced and bared his teeth in pain. His face was flushed, and the skin of his neck and throat was bright red.

Tears stung Jerico's own eyes. He couldn't bear to see Andy hurt like this.

He dropped to his haunches at his side and gently took his free hand. "I'm here," he said softly.

"Jerico." Andy turned in his direction. The water splattered down his cheek.

"Keep still," the black woman said firmly. She took hold of his chin and turned his head back towards her. "We have to keep this up for fifteen minutes." She passed an empty bottle to someone beside her and accepted a full one. Twisting the cap, she said, "Keep your eyes wide open."

Andy used his fingers to pry both eyelids open, and the women resumed the slow, steady pour of water. Andy's clothes were saturated as it ran over his chest and onto his shorts. There was a towel in his lap, and even that was drenched.

Jerico turned to Jake. "Do you have any more towels? He's drowning in this."

Jake nodded. "I'll be right back."

"Did anyone call the police?" he asked the people standing by.

A man in his forties nodded. "They're sending someone to take statements."

"What about an ambulance? Why aren't the paramedics here?"

"They said there was no need," the man answered. "They said to administer the eye baths and call them back if he didn't get better."

"No *need*?" he yelled incredulously. "How the hell can they say that when he's had an unknown substance thrown in his face. I'm calling them now."

"Calm down," Andy said. He showed staggering resolve, keeping his head still while the woman poured the water over his eyes. He spluttered and caught his breath. "I'm fine...really. If it was anything worse than alcohol, my skin would be raw by now."

Jerico struggled to keep calm. He felt so fucking helpless. He hated to see anyone in pain, let alone someone he cared so deeply for. "This is fucked up," he said, his voice barely above a whisper.

Andy heard and squeezed his hand in encouragement.

The woman emptied the last of the bottle and checked her watch. "I make that about eighteen minutes. I think we can stop if you feel all right."

Jake handed him a wad of fresh towels. Andy pressed one to his face. His chest expanded as he took deep, noisy breaths. Jerico took another of the towels and wrapped it around his shoulders, holding him gently.

Eventually, Andy lowered the towel. He sniffed as he blinked carefully, turning his head to look around the room. "I'm okay," he said at last. "I mean, my eyes are sore, but I can see. It's like when you've been swimming underwater. It's kind of raw, but I don't think there's any damage done."

"Thank Christ." Jerico hugged him tighter.

"Thanks, Lizzie," Andy said to the woman who'd given him first aid. Then to everyone else. "Thank you for your help."

There was a sense of relief as everyone collectively exhaled.

"I think I need a drink," Lizzie said.

"We all do after that," Jake said, heading to the counter. He began un-capping bottles of beer and lining them up on the counter. "Help yourselves...whoever needs it."

"Are you sure you're okay?" Jerico said, while the others started on the refreshments.

Andy rubbed his eyes again with the towel and nodded. "Shocked more than anything. It could have been worse."

"It should never have happened. This is my fault. I've put you in danger. If I hadn't come back into your life, you wouldn't have been a target. I'm so sorry."

"You don't know that any of that is true, and at this point, I don't want to hear it, either. I'm just glad that you're here."

Over the next ten minutes, Andy gradually improved, and his confidence seemingly returned. He put the damp towels down and got to his feet. Jerico stayed right by his side, offering his arm and weight should he need someone to lean on. Andy kept looking about the room to test his eyesight and assured everyone that he thought it was getting better.

Jerico didn't want to say it out loud, but it pissed him off that the police had yet to arrive. What if Dean had really thrown acid in Andy's face or attacked him with a knife — or hit him with a car? Were they so fucking useless that they couldn't recognise an emergency when it was called in?

A woman arrived a few minutes later. Though they hadn't met yet, Jerico knew from how upset she was that she had to be Andy's mother. She ran crying towards him and almost slipped on the wet tiles. Jerico caught her before she lost her balance then she was on top of Andy, smothering him in her embrace.

"Where's the ambulance? Why aren't you in the hospital?" she asked between sobs.

"Mam, I've already been over this. I'm fine. I don't need one," he assured her.

"I'd feel much better if you were checked out professionally," Jerico said.

Mari looked at him, her own eyes bloodshot and teary, and she nodded. "So would I. I'm going to take you to the hospital. My car is at the hotel. I'll fetch it now."

Andy gripped her arm. "I don't want to go. It will be a waste of everyone's time. I'm okay. I promise you. If I thought for a second that I needed it, I would go."

"Is it true that someone attacked you in the street? Threw acid in your face?"

"It wasn't acid. It was spirits. We've rinsed it all out."

"Then where are the damn police? Why aren't they here? You were attacked. Is anyone even out there looking for the fucker who did this to you?"

Despite his concerns about the situation, Jerico took an instant liking to Andy's mother. She was saying out loud all the things he was holding in.

"He'll be long gone," Andy said. "He was on a bike."

"A bike?" She turned to stare at Jerico. "Like the man who petrol-bombed your window? Oh, my God, this is related, isn't it? What the hell are you involved in? What have you dragged my son into?"

Jerico nodded. "It's the same man. I'm sure of it."

Her lips retracted in an expression of pure anger. "You're sure of it, are you? And what the hell are you so sure of?" She was shouting now. "And when were you going to tell Andy he was in danger? What next? Is he going to be doused in petrol?"

Jerico couldn't argue with her or defend himself, because what Mari said was correct. Dean Ferguson's deranged feud with Jerico had followed him all the way to Nyemouth, and now those close to him were in direct danger.

After what he'd done so far, Dean was obviously capable of anything.

Chapter Fifteen

Andy sat in the living room, his feet propped on the coffee table, with Patches in his lap, gazing at him with concern. He'd always been a kind, empathic cat and knew when Andy needed comfort. Mari was in the kitchen taking snipes at a defensive Jerico.

"You knew this guy was after you, and you did nothing to protect my son," she snapped.

She'd been making the same argument for over an hour.

After returning to the house and getting Andy settled on the sofa, Jerico had told them everything about his stalker, Dean Ferguson—how it had started as a feud on a TV show and escalated to the point where Dean had set fire to the restaurant Jerico had been working at. Jerico had gone into detail, revealing the lengths Dean had gone to in his harassment campaign, before progressing to arson. It had last years.

The police didn't know where Dean was, though Jerico was convinced he was here in Nyemouth.

While Jerico and his mother continued to snipe, Andy took out his phone and did an image search for Dean Ferguson and *Top Cook*. The photos were from ten years ago, of a slightly built young man with immature features. *Is that the guy I saw today? Can't be sure.* Andy hadn't seen enough of him. He hadn't been paying attention until the moment the attacker rode over, then it had been too late. All he had seen was a cap, sunglasses and a medical face mask. That should have given him a clue that something was off. Not many people wore them out in the public these days. The guy might have been little. If he pushed himself, his first impression might have been that the figure on the bike was a slim teenager, but Andy didn't trust his own recollection. He could be projecting what he wanted to see.

He searched for more recent photos of Dean. They were almost five years old, from the time of his trial for the fire. Because of Jerico's fame and their history of the TV show, it had been well covered by the press, and there were plenty of pictures of Dean going in and out of court. He hadn't changed much from his *Top Cook* days—slim built with short brown hair. Andy was surprised to read that he'd been thirty at the time of the trial. He looked like a teen.

After four days of evidence, the jury had been unanimous and found him guilty after just seventeen minutes of deliberation.

He hated Jerico enough to start a fire in a restaurant. How deep is that hatred now, after losing his freedom and serving time in prison?

Although Andy had not seen his face today, he had to agree with Jerico and conclude that Dean was the man who had attacked him.

He put down the phone. It strained his already sensitive eyes to focus on the screen. He gave Patches a gentle stroke behind the ear. The cat purred and leaned in for more.

"If he knows you are seeing Andy, then he'll likely know where he lives," Mari charged Jerico, before turning towards Andy. "It's not safe for you to stay here. I think you should move in with me until the police catch him."

Andy kept his voice calm, refusing to engage in their battle. "I'm not moving out. This is my home. And I won't leave Patches, anyway."

"Patches can come with you."

"You've got two rottweilers. They drive me round the bend. I'm not forcing this old boy to share space with them."

"Then Jacob can take him in for a few days. They adore each other. He'll be happy to have him."

"I'm not discussing it any further. I'm staying put. Now, if either of you want to do something more constructive than arguing, my tea has gone cold."

"I'll get it," Jerico said. He grabbed the kettle and filled it.

"It's the least you can bloody do," Mari muttered.

"Mam, stop it. Come sit down. You need to relax, too."

She pulled a petulant face but came through to the living room and sat in the armchair. Jerico followed to collect the empty teacups.

"How are you now?" he asked.

"I'm fine," Andy assured him. "It doesn't even hurt anymore. My eyes are tired, though."

"It could have been so much worse," Mari grumbled.

Andy sighed, "But it isn't. So that's something to be grateful for, eh?"

Mari still wore her grey trouser suit from the hotel. She took off her black high heels and removed her jacket before slouching back in the armchair.

"You look knackered," Andy told her. "Maybe you should go home to bed." He glanced at the clock, shocked to discover it was only eight-thirty-five. It felt like so much later.

"I'll have another cup of tea with you before I go. We need to talk about your security first."

"That's a bit dramatic, isn't it?"

"You mum's right," Jerico said, leaning over the kitchen counter. "I hate to say this, but you are in danger. I know what Dean's like. There's nothing he won't stoop to. Today is proof of that."

Andy knew they meant well, but it bugged him that they were treating him like a five-year-old. "I'll handle this myself."

"I know," Jerico said kindly. "But you need to take precautions, too."

The kettle came to the boil, and Jerico set about making fresh tea. Andy was glad to let the subject drop for a moment. "There are biscuits in the top cupboard," he said.

"Have you eaten anything?" his mother asked. "Want me to make you something? I could knock up a bowl of pasta or order a takeaway."

"I'm not hungry. I just want you to relax. You've been running on nerves these last few hours. It's not good for you."

She sighed and raised a tired smile. "I think you're right."

Jerico brought through three mugs of tea, retrieved the biscuits from the kitchen and joined them in the living room, taking the second armchair across from Andy. He still wore his black kitchen tunic and trousers from work. He sipped his tea and sat back in the chair. "Now," he said, "we were talking about security."

There was clearly going to be no escape.

"Yes," Mari said. Suddenly they were both on the same side.

"Given that you're the real target, I would think you're the one who needs to beef up his security," Andy said.

"I realise that, and I intend to. We've already got a night watchman in the restaurant, but I'm going to make that twenty-four-hour cover. And we'll need to increase security for the opening at the weekend."

"Richie can help you with that," Mari said.

"Who is Richie?"

"Mam's partner," Andy told him.

"Richie runs his own security firm," she explained. "He's got a great team. He'll be able to provide you with all the cover you need."

"At such short notice?"

"Don't worry. I'll make sure he does." Mari picked up her phone and clicked out a text message.

"Great," Jerico said. "That takes care of the business. Now we need to consider your personal security."

Patches let out a small meow of agreement.

Andy laughed. They were all in on it. "I'm not going to have a bodyguard following me around. I manage a hotel. I'm not Whitney Houston."

"I'm not talking about that kind of thing, but you need to take precautions until Dean is arrested," Jerico said.

"And what do you suggest?"

"You shouldn't be alone, for a start. I don't mean at home. If you lock these doors, this place is secure enough, but no more walking around town. Do you have a car?"

"I do, but I'm not going to drive to work when it takes a few minutes to walk there. I could be at the hotel in the time it takes me to get the car out of the garage."

"It should only be for a few days, maybe not even that long."

"And if you refuse, then I'll have to take you to work and bring you home myself." Mari didn't stop texting as she spoke. "Which would you prefer?"

"All right." They had beaten him into submission. Their concern was sweet, but he didn't need it. He was aware of the danger and wouldn't be caught out by Psycho Dean again. "I'll take the car and fuck the environment."

"The environment will still be here this time next week. If you have another run-in with this nutter, you might not be." Mari put her phone on the arm of the chair. "Right, Richie will meet you at the restaurant at ten-thirty tomorrow to go through your requirements. And don't worry. I've told him I want this job at a family rate." She turned to Andy. "And I've just ordered you a personal safety alarm. It will be delivered tomorrow. I've given instructions to leave it with Jacob if you're not in. Once it arrives, you're to keep it on you at all times. Understood?"

She made him feel like he was ten again. "All right. I will."

"You had better. And keep your phone fully charged and with you all the time, too."

"When is anyone ever without their phone?" he asked, exasperated.

"Consider it a gentle reminder."

The conversation circled around in a similar vein until they had exhausted themselves. At quarter to ten,

Mari announced that she was done in. She gathered her things together. Her car was parked out in the front. Before leaving, she fixed Jerico in her steely gaze.

"Are you staying?" she asked.

"Yeah," Jerico said, then looked at Andy. "If it's all right with you."

Despite the tension and anxiety of the last few hours, a reassuring warmth spread through him. He wouldn't admit it out loud, but he didn't want to be alone tonight. "Yes. Thanks."

Mari gathered him a tight hug and sought more assurances that he would lock the door behind her, take care of himself and phone the police if he heard anything suspicious through the night. He swore he would and waved her off until her car disappeared down the hill.

"Your mum is great," Jerico said, as they stepped back inside and locked up.

"Really? I thought she was going to rip you a new arsehole at one point."

Jerico chuckled. "She's a fierce momma. She's just looking out for you. I can't blame her for that."

Jerico wrapped his strong arms around Andy and held him tight to his chest. Andy surrendered, laying his head on his shoulder, enjoying the beat of their hearts against each other.

"I'm so sorry for bringing you into all this shit," Jerico said.

"Stop apologising. You've been dealing with this loser for the best part of ten years. You don't have to face him on your own anymore."

"I don't want you to get hurt."

"It won't happen again. He caught me by surprise today. That's his one and only chance. I'll be ready for the bastard the next time."

They unwound with a quick whisky before clearing things up for the night.

"Do you mind if I have a shower before bed?" Jerico asked, indicating his work clothes. "I'm pretty stinky under here."

"You know where it is. The fresh towels are in the airing cupboard at the top of the stairs."

Andy loaded the dishwasher and gave Patches his supper. Before heading upstairs, he double-checked that all the doors and windows were locked on the ground floor. He stared out of the living room window. It was only ten o'clock. The sun had set but the sky was still light. The garden and the road beyond were both empty. There were no shadows for Dean Ferguson to hide in. Andy drew the curtains and went up to bed.

Jerico was in the shower, his broad body outlined through the frosted glass. Andy washed his face and brushed his teeth. Jerico shut off the water, and Andy handed him a towel. Despite the trauma of the day, he couldn't help appreciating the beauty of his build...how water trickled through the damp curls of his chest and down his belly.

"That feels so much better," Jerico said, rubbing the towel over his head, then along his torso.

The bathroom was small. Andy stepped out to give him the room he needed. "Help yourself to anything you need. My toiletries are all in the cupboard beneath the sink. You'll find a packet of spare toothbrushes in there, too."

He retreated to the bedroom and checked the view outside one more time before closing the curtains. He switched on the lamp at the side of the bed and stripped naked before sliding beneath the cool covers. Though he was physically exhausted, he wondered if sleep would be easy tonight. His mind was all over the place, considering the annoying 'what if's?'.

Let it go for now. Dean wanted to give me a shock. If he'd wanted to cause serious harm, he could have done it. This is part of a plan to rattle Jerico and derail the opening. I need to look out for Jerico. This is likely to escalate in the coming days.

Jerico came out of the bathroom, naked. His big soft cock waggled as he dried his hair vigorously with the towel. Andy's gaze roved all over, taking in every wonderful line and curve of his body. He lifted the bedcovers.

"Don't waste time over there. You'll get cold."

Jerico beamed, crossed the room and slipped into bed. He smelled wonderfully fresh and clean. The scent of shampoo was strong on his hair. They lay on their sides. Andy pulled him closed and hooked his leg over Jerico's bare thigh.

"Thanks for staying."

Jerico's tiger eyes glistened in the glow of the bedside light. "I wasn't going to leave you alone."

"Shit, I just remembered. We had a reservation for dinner tonight that we didn't cancel."

"I dealt with it."

"You did?"

"When you were giving your statement to the police, I went along and explained. They were fine and said we can rebook any time."

"Crikey, you think of everything."

Jerico snuggled into the pillow. "I guess it comes from a decade of working in kitchens. I'm always aware of their bottom line."

"I was looking forward to it, too — our first proper date."

Jerico slipped his hand along Andy's torso, coming to rest on his hip. "If you discount all those dates from our past."

Andy tilted his hips, leaning into Jerico's touch. "I don't remember us really going on dates, not in the traditional sense—drinks at the crew bar and a few lunches ashore when our work patterns allowed it."

"Mmm, you could be right. I hadn't thought about it like that. In that case, we need to go out for a real date sometime, when everything is settled."

"That will be wonderful, though I doubt you'll have many nights free after Friday."

"Once the staff are trained and the kitchen is up and running, I have every intention of taking one, if not two, evenings off a week. That might not be until the end of the first month, but I know how important time off is. It's tempting when it's your own business to work all day every day, but I don't want to be like that. I want to have a life away from work. And now, you've given me something else to focus on apart from the restaurant."

Andy shuffled across the bed, rolled Jerico onto his back and crawled on top. He lay over Jerico, their bodies connected at the chest, belly, groin and thighs. Jerico brought his hands around him and settled them on his arse.

"I'll give you all the support you need," Andy said. He placed his lips on top of Jerico's. They opened their mouths, their tongues connected and they got lost in the kiss. In a few seconds their cocks were hard and rubbing together. Jerico's grip on his buttocks became more persistent.

"Are you sure you're up for this?" Jerico murmured against his lips. "You've had a bruising day."

"Your psycho stalker robbed me of our date. He's not going to take your cock from me, too."

They gripped each other tighter and giggled, like they were young men in their twenties again, without a worry in the world.

For the rest of the night, they would keep it that way.

Chapter Sixteen

Mari's boyfriend Richie Goldman met Jerico at the restaurant promptly at ten-thirty the next morning. He was a muscular black man in his early forties. He was dressed well in dark trousers and a navy polo shirt with the logo of Goldman's Security emblazoned proudly on the left breast. The short sleeves revealed impressive biceps and powerful forearms. Richie struck him as polite, professional and strong. Handsome, too. Andy's mother had good taste.

"Thanks for coming," Jerico said, leading him to the office on the first floor.

"I'm glad to be of help. I love what you've done with this place."

"You've been here before?"

"A couple of years ago. One of the previous owners had a problem with vandals while the premises stood empty. We provided them with nighttime security."

So, he was already familiar with the building. Even better.

"Can I get you something to drink?" Jerico asked, indicating he take a seat.

"I'm fine, thank you." Richie sat, opened his leather briefcase and extracted a document, before placing the case on the floor. Straight down to business. Jerico liked him even more.

Jerico sat on the other side of the desk. "I take it Mari has filled you in on what's been happening."

Richie's smile was easy and confident. "It's better that I hear it direct from you. You're the client, and I want to deliver the security that suits you best. You'd be surprised how much the details can change when a third party recounts a story."

Jerico tried to keep it brief and to the point, but summarising ten years of torment wasn't easy. He stuck to the current facts. Dean Ferguson was somewhere in the area and unaccounted for and had an eye on sabotaging the opening of the restaurant.

"I'm not sure he'd be so bold as to try anything on the first night. We'll have press and media coverage. It might be too public for him. But I wouldn't be surprised if he tries to sabotage things within the first week."

"If he's as unstable as he appears to be, I wouldn't rule out anything. Until the police catch up with him, you need to prepare for anything at any time."

"I agree. We've got security while the building is empty at night, but I want to step it up around the restaurant for the first week at least. We can review it on a weekly basis from there."

Richie made some notes. "There's only one entrance to the public, at the front?"

Jerico nodded. "And an exit at the back, through the kitchen."

"Fire escape?"

"There's one on the left of the dining room, but it won't be open unless there's an emergency. The only real way in is through the front or the back."

"Good. And the guestlist for your opening? I take it you don't know them all personally?"

"No."

"So, if he wants to come inside, it's possible he could get in through the guest list."

"I hadn't thought of that."

"Okay, here's what I suggest. For this weekend, I would put two guards on the front door. Everyone who comes in is bag-searched and checked with a metal detector. Your VIP guest won't like it, but if this guy is dangerous, it's a risk you can't take. I would put a third guard at the back door, and a fourth to patrol the exterior and help inside if an incident occurs. After the weekend, this could be reviewed, and you may be able to go down to one guard at the front and another at the back door."

Jerico was astonished. He hadn't considered any of this. With the practicalities of the opening, getting his staff trained up, making sure they had all their ingredients on hand and plenty of booze in stock, until this week he hadn't given a thought to security.

"I don't know what to say. It sounds...heavy handed."

Richie's gaze was unwavering. "Only you can judge that. You've had problems with this guy for ten years. He's acted on his threats before. How serious a risk do you consider him to be? This is your first restaurant in your own name. How jealous is he likely to be of that? He only has to throw another one of his petrol bombs through the window on your first night and all this incredible work that you've done will have been for nothing."

Jerico sat in silence, weighing up Richie's words. He got no impression that Richie was hyping the stakes to secure a bigger job for himself. He'd already explained to Jerico on arrival that he would knock a sizeable discount from the final bill.

"You're right," he said at last. "Dean Ferguson has always been insanely jealous. I can't put anything past him. Let's do everything you've suggested. I want it all."

"I think you're making the right decision," Richie said, adding notes to his document.

They discussed the practicalities of the arrangement before Jerico took him on a full tour of the building, checking out all the weak points in his security.

"I don't see any CCTV," Richie remarked.

"Couldn't make the dates work," Jerico said. "The earliest we can get cameras installed is the beginning of next month."

"We can work around that. My team will all be wearing body cams, so if something should go wrong, we'll have a record of it."

"Christ, there's so much to think about." Jerico raked his fingers through his hair.

Richie put a reassuring hand on his arm. "All you need to think about now is your business. Leave the security side of this to me and my team. We're on board to take all that worry away. It's our job. Now you can concentrate on yours."

"You've no idea how glad I am. Last night, I thought there was a good chance Mari was going to punch me. Now I'm so grateful for her recommending you."

Richie laughed, no longer the serious security manager, just a regular guy. "She would have taken a swing if she thought you deserved it. She's a tough one."

"I'm starting to learn that. Andy is lucky to have her on his side. Have you been together long?"

"Getting on to four years," Richie said. "Though I've known her a lot longer than that. I used to follow her round the clubs when I was younger. Never thought I'd end up living with her, though. I couldn't believe it when she asked me out."

"You must be doing something right...four years."

"We'd be married by now if I had my way, but she won't hear of it. Said she tried it once and never again. I live in hope that she'll back down on that one of these days."

Jerico wondered how much Andy was like his mother. He used to talk about her a lot during their cruise days, and he would call her as often as he could. The phone charges on the ship had been extortionate, but Andy always made sure to get in touch with his mum whenever they had gone ashore. He couldn't remember him ever mentioning his dad much. Jerico assumed he'd been out of the picture from when Andy had been a kid.

It said a lot about Mari that she had been the one to ask Richie out but then rejected his proposals of marriage. He guessed that when the time was right, Mari would be the one to pop the question.

Jerico and Richie shook hands on the arrangement and agreed that Richie would come back with his team on Thursday evening for a walk-through before the opening on Friday night. Even with the discount, it would be a big expense that Jerico and Rafiq hadn't budgeted for, but the costs would be even greater if Dean managed to sabotage their launch.

Jerico spent the rest of the morning in the kitchen with his staff, and the time flew by. He lost himself in work and managed to blot out all thoughts of Dean for a few hours. The police called after two to give him an update, which amounted to nothing. They had no clue of Dean's current whereabout. He had transferred substantial amounts of money out of his bank nine months ago and hadn't accessed the accounts since. The money itself had been moved several times until they had lost all trace of it.

Dean's parents had died when he'd been young, and he'd been raised by his grandparents. When they were later killed in a car accident, Dean had inherited everything, enough money to set him up for life. Having spent the last few years in jail, that money had only been gathering interest.

It was obvious to Jerico that he'd been planning this the whole time he'd been inside. To have successfully set up a new identity and bank accounts that the police were currently unable to trace took time, resources and connections. Now he was in Nyemouth, well-funded and completely beneath the radar.

"We'll find him," the police officer had told him. "We'll be able to trace the money eventually. It will just take time."

Time was the one thing Jerico was short of. They were four days away from the launch. If they hadn't caught up with Dean by then, Jerico was likely fucked.

The afternoon took a turn for the better when Andy arrived after three with takeaway coffee.

"I knew you'd be working hard and unlikely to take a break," he said. He looked mighty fine in his dark suit trousers and an open-necked white shirt. Andy had insisted he was going to work that morning, claiming that he would be safer in a busy hotel than by himself at home. Jerico hadn't liked it, but he'd been unable to argue with the logic.

"What about you?" Jerico said. "Have you eaten?"

Andy shrugged his shoulders. "Who has time for food?"

"We do," Jerico stated, guiding him to a table, well away from the window. No point in offering Dean a clear target. He kissed Andy on the lips as he sat.

From the kitchen, he asked one of the chefs to put together a mixed platter of lunchtime staples. Jerico was certain they had the recipes refined to perfection, but it was always good to get another opinion. He returned to the table and popped the lid off the takeaway coffee.

"This smells great. Where did you get it from? Your hotel?"

"God, no. The stuff we serve is decent, but it's not worth taking out. I picked these up from The Seagull Café. I wanted to drop by to thank them for what they did for me yesterday."

Jerico sipped appreciatively. The coffee tasted as good as it smelled—strong and intensely rich. Suddenly he stared at Andy. "Hang on. How did you get there? Or get here? Have you brought the car?"

"Of course I haven't. It's no more than a few minutes door to door."

Jerico was exasperated. "Andy—"

"Relax. I walked over the bridge with our food and beverage manager. The part I did on my own was from the café to here."

"That's all the bastard needs. You should know that."

Andy rummaged in his pocket and pulled out a slim, plastic device, no bigger than a cigarette lighter. "My personal alarm. Jacob brought them in earlier. A pack of three arrived today, thanks to my mam. If anyone even looks at me the wrong way, I just need to set this off."

"What does it do?"

"Makes a siren noise."

"I doubt that will deter Dean. You need some mace spray, too."

"This is enough. I drove to work like you wanted, but I'm not going to drive a few hundred yards for a coffee. And I'm not going to hide."

Jerico didn't want to argue. Andy was being reckless, but how many years had it been before he took Dean to be a serious threat himself? If he really wanted to scupper whatever Dean had planned, all he had to do was delay the opening of the restaurant, and there was no chance of him doing that. *No fucking way*. It would give the twisted little bastard exactly what he wanted.

"I'll walk you back to the hotel after lunch."

"And who will escort you back here afterwards?" Andy asked lightly. "You're at an even greater risk than I am. You're the one he really hates. Don't you see how ludicrous it is?"

Jerico slumped in surrender. "Okay, when we reach the hotel, you can give me one of those alarms from your pack of three."

They both chuckled. "Deal."

The food came out of the kitchen. Jerico swelled with pride as it was presented and noted the delighted expression on Andy's face. There were bowls of hummus and baba ghanoj, marinated and grilled chicken strips, lamb skewers, roasted vegetable mash, sauteed greens and a plate of flat breads. Andy leaned in to inhale the delicious aroma.

"Wow," Andy said.

"These are staples from the lunch menu, which starts on Saturday," Jerico told him. "Simple stuff, but when it's done well, it's as grand as our premier options."

"Can I just dive in?"

Jerico gestured for him to go ahead.

Andy grabbed an empty plate and filled it with chicken and lamb, before tearing a flatbread into pieces and dipping it into the hummus.

"Mmm," Andy said, closing his eyes and clearly savouring the flavours.

Jerico loved watching people eat and to see the pleasure his food gave them. It was doubly special to see how much Andy enjoyed it. He filled his own plate with a sample of everything.

"I didn't realise I was so hungry," Andy said, when he'd finished the first serving. He took another flat bread and went in for more.

"You like it?"

"You're kidding, aren't you? I love it. This is fantastic." He spread more hummus over the bread then rolled it around a juicy piece of chicken before taking a huge bite. He chewed and swallowed. "I won't need any dinner tonight, which is just as well. I might need to work late."

"Is your mum working today?"

Andy nodded, his mouth full again.

"I'll get the kitchen to make up a box to takeaway, as a thank you to her for hooking me up with Richie."

Andy wiped his mouth. "It worked out okay?"

"I think so. He knows what he's talking about, so I'm leaving all the security to him. Whatever he thinks is required is what we'll have."

"Brilliant. Richie is the best you can get. And now you're in safe hands, you can forget about Dean and focus completely on your launch." Andy pulled chunks of lamb off a skewer with his fingers. "And when you're serving food as delicious as this, you don't have to worry about a thing. Nyemouth won't know what's hit when you open."

Jerico's smile was only partly genuine. He wanted to share Andy's confidence, and he did feel more secure after his meeting with Richie than he had before. But he was the only one who had experience with Dean, and after years of abuse, he'd learned to expect the unexpected.

He hoped he could count on Richie and his team to keep his staff, customers and loved ones safe.

If not, the outcome would be disastrous.

Chapter Seventeen

Jacob Chisholm washed up the plates and pan from his dinner and left them to dry on the drainer. There was no point bothering with the dishwasher anymore. When he was on his own, it took him the best part of a week to fill it. He dried his hands and walked through to the living room. It was a beautiful evening. With nothing else planned, he decided he would take a book into the front garden with a nice glass of whisky and enjoy the balmy weather while it lasted. Dominic Melton had given him an advance copy of his latest novel on the weekend. Jacob was only a third of the way through and already hooked. He couldn't wait to find out what happened next.

When Dominic had been his neighbour, they'd been such close friends. Now he lived on the other side of the river with his husband Arnie and stepson AJ. Jacob had also known Arnie for most of his life, and the two were perfect for each other.

He still saw Dominic two or three times a week at the lifeboat station, but Jacob missed the days when he used to live next door. The nights they'd spend together, setting the world to rights over a good bottle of single malt. Jacob adored his current neighbours, Matt and Jake on one side and Andy on the other, but he still missed those boozy nights with Dominic. He'd been lucky in the years he'd lived up here on South Bank, to be surrounded by the very best company.

As he bent to retrieve the large format paperback and the coffee, his phone rang. It was Andy.

"Hi," he answered. "Don't tell me, you need me to feed the cat?"

"Do you mind?" Andy said. "I'm stuck at work. Going to be here for at least a couple of more hours."

"You know I don't. I'll go around now. But you work too hard."

"My deputy manager and concierge both called in sick. There's no one else."

"Do you want me to sort you out something to eat for later? I've got some fresh mackerel. If you let me know when you're ready to come home, I can grill them and bring them around."

"Thanks, Jacob, but I've already eaten. I went to see Jerico earlier, and he filled me up at the restaurant then gave me a huge amount of food to bring over for the staff here."

"If you change your mind, just call." Jacob loved looking after people. When Annabelle had been alive, they'd been the most sociable couple in Nyemouth. His wife had loved to entertain and cook. In her later years, when she'd been unable to, he'd taken over the reins. She had enjoyed nothing more than sitting in the garden, chatting with friends while Jacob kept them replenished. With her passing, he'd felt an obligation to her memory to continue her tradition.

"I hope you're free on Friday night," Andy said. "I haven't had a chance to ask you, with everything that's been going on, but Jerico has given me a table at the restaurant for the opening. My mam will be there, and I was going to ask Matt, Jake, Arnie and Dominic. Will you join us?"

Jacob was stunned into silence. Why would they want an old man like him at such a fancy event?

"Are you still there?" Andy asked.

"Yes," he croaked, overwhelmed. Then, finding his voice, "Are you sure?"

"Of course I'm sure," Andy said. "Why do you think I'm asking? I'd love you to come with me. We'll be a little South Bank posse. Apart from my mam, we've all lived up there at some point, and she spends so much time at my place she might as well class it as her second address."

Jacob managed to laugh and was glad Andy wasn't there to see how flushed his face had become. "I'd like that very much. Thank you. I don't know what to say."

"You already have, and I'm glad. It will be a great night. We won't see much of Jerico. He'll be busy in the kitchen or talking to the press and VIPs, but we'll have our own little party."

Jacob smiled to himself when he came off the phone. A celebrity restaurant opening. That was a first. And a huge honour. *What should I wear?* He'd bought a new suit two years ago when Arnie Walker had invited him to a premiere screening of a TV show he'd starred in. It hadn't been out of the wardrobe since. That would have to do, though he doubted there was time to have it dry cleaned before Friday. He'd have to get it out and see if it still fit first, then maybe he could ask them to rush it through at the cleaners. If he told them what it was for, he was sure they'd make allowances.

Later, he told himself. He had to give Patches his supper first.

Still smiling, he collected the keys for Andy's place from the hook. He locked his own front door before walking down the path. When he'd first moved here with his wife, over fifty years ago, they hadn't worried about things like that. They could visit their neighbours for a couple of hours and never think about security. Nyemouth was a far different place now—murder, assault, home invasions. He doubted Annabelle would recognise it with all the terrible things that went on these days.

Like his wife, Jacob had always been a positive person. It was too easy to get bogged down in bad news. See the best in everything... That's how he wanted to enjoy the rest of his life.

Patches was sunning himself in Andy's front garden. He perked up at the sound of the gate opening and got to his feet, stretching before sauntering over. The old boy rarely wandered beyond the boundary of Andy's property, but there was a cat flap in the front door to allow him in and out as he pleased.

"You look like you're enjoying yourself," Jacob said cheerfully.

Patches chirped a firm confirmation.

"Ready for something to eat?"

This time a loud meow and a leg brush were the positive reply.

"Come on then," Jacob said. "Let's see what your daddy has left for you tonight."

He unlocked Andy's front door and went inside.

The old man let himself into Andy's house, and the cat followed at his heels.

Dean Ferguson, unrecognisable with a baseball cap, fake blond ponytail and from-the-bottle suntan, watched from across the street. If anyone should look at him, they would see a passing tourist enjoying a cigarette and the view before heading back to his B&B or holiday let. His gaze wandered from the bay, up and down the street and towards the sky, but his focus was all on Andy's house.

He'd been waiting for Jerico's fuckbuddy to return from work.

In the backpack, slung casually over his shoulder, he had cable ties, rope and a six-inch serrated hunting knife. His plans were flexible. He had no idea whether Andy would come home alone or with Jerico in tow.

The old man going in to feed the cat meant Andy was working late again.

Or spending the night with Jerico.

Jerico's apartment, situated within a communal building, was more secure and difficult to access. Andy's house was a far easier target. The dumb bastard left his front door open most of the time he was home. Dean could walk in undetected, and Andy wouldn't even know until his blade slashed across his jugular.

He couldn't make up his mind whether he wanted to kill Andy or not. He flip-flopped all the time. When he woke up that morning, he'd decided, yes, he would take him out. The bond Andy had formed with Jerico seemed stronger every day. The perfect way to hurt the bastard would be to destroy the thing he loved.

Killing held no distaste for Dean. Quite the opposite. He'd come to enjoy it over the years. Even better when he got away with it. It was sickening that he'd spent time in jail for a piddling fire, when he'd been responsible for three deaths already. Not his useless mother… Her addictions had been the end of her. Dead at twenty-two in her junkie boyfriend's flat. She'd lain in the bedroom with a needle in her arm for three days before anyone had noticed she was dead. Nobody missed her, least of all Dean.

When he'd been taken in by his grandparents at six years old, his young life had finally found some stability. Until Uncle Eddie, kicked out by his wife, moved in with them when he was ten. His mother's problem had been heroin, her brother's was the bottle. The peaceful home was suddenly filled with anger, noise and violence. The abuse he suffered was verbal, until he was thirteen, when Eddie began to use his fists on the teenager.

The bastard's drinking had worked in Dean's favour. They were alone in the house one night when Eddie had stumbled to bed pissed as a fart. It had only taken a firm shove when he reached the top of the stairs, and Eddie had toppled backwards, breaking his neck in the fall. There was so much alcohol swilling around his system that no one suspected anything other than an accident.

Except his grandmother… After Eddie's death, she started to look at Dean in a different way. It was a pity the old bag hadn't taken more notice of what was going on with him before her son met his end.

His grandparents were a little harder to deal with, but it had all worked out in the end. They were driving home late at night from one of their gala dinners, when a stolen car ran them off the road, killing them both instantly. The car was later found burned out, and the driver never discovered. As their only surviving relative, Dean had inherited everything at nineteen, including the house and a healthy insurance payout.

He'd been tempted since then. In prison, a baby-faced, slightly built man had attracted the wrong kind of attention, but Dean was no idiot. There had been no way to dispose of his tormentors without getting caught. He wanted his sentence to be over as fast as possible, and that didn't involve going down for the murder of a scumbag armed robber. They could wait. He'd kept tabs on all of those who'd crossed him, knew when they'd be getting released and when. They were problems for another day.

His top priority had always been Jerico Osman. He would kill Jerico eventually, but before then, he wanted to torment him in the worst way possible.

The alcohol attack on his boyfriend had rattled him. After a rapid image change, Dean had hung around to watch the aftermath. He'd seen the concern on Jerico's face as he rushed to be with Andy. The more Jerico hurt, the better Dean felt.

The old man shut the front door behind him. He was obviously a lot more security conscious than Andy.

Who was he, anyway? More importantly, what was his relationship with Jerico?

If a splash of vodka in Andy's face had caused him so much anguish, how would Jerico feel when his lover came home to find the old man and the cat dead in his kitchen?

Dean flushed with glee. It was a great idea — one of his best yet.

Checking to see that there was nothing coming in either direction, he crossed the road.

"How does beef in gravy sound?" Jacob asked, inspecting the selection of pouches available in Andy's cupboard.

Patches meowed a yes.

"Beef it is."

Jacob opened the packet and spooned half of the rich-smelling food into Patches' feeding bowl. He had no idea where Andy bought the cat food from, but it was very high quality. It looked better than a lot of the tinned food Jacob had in his own cupboards.

"I think your daddy might spoil you."

Patches rubbed against his leg.

"Careful not to trip me up," he said, shuffling along the side of the counter to reach his feeding mat. Jacob's back and knees ached in protest as he bent to put the bowl down.

Patches stuffed his face in the bowl and scoffed like he hadn't been fed in weeks.

Jacob straightened and smiled as he watched the cat make short work of the food. For an old boy, he still had quite the appetite, not unlike Jacob himself. He ran a bowl of hot water and added washing up liquid. He'd wait until Patches had finished and clean up after him. It would save Andy a job when he got in later.

Jacob turned off the tap and looked out of the kitchen window. Like most of the residents on the terrace, Andy had created a cosy sitting area out back. Hardly anyone used them because the sun shone on the rear of the property for such a short time each day and was blocked by the high cliff face behind it. Unlike the fronts of the houses, the backs were private, and if they had sufficient outdoor heating, it was nice to dine out there in the summer.

A sudden movement caught his eye. It happened so fast, Jacob wasn't even sure what he'd noticed.

Then it came again. The latch in the back gate lifted and fell.

Someone was trying to get it.

They would have a tough time, as the gate was bolted at the top and bottom. But if whoever was there was intent on robbery, they would likely try all the gates in the street.

Not while I'm around.

Jacob shuffled through the keys on the set Andy had given him until he found the one for the back door.

As he looked out again, a hand reached over the gate, feeling it's way until it found the top bolt.

The cheeky little bugger. They were not intent on giving up easily.

Jacob unlocked the door and stepped into the yard. The hand disappeared over the gate.

"Hello," he called out. "Can I help you?"

Silence. He hadn't expected an answer.

He crossed the yard to inspect the gate. Patches followed him out, head and tail held high.

The prowler had managed to unlock the top bolt.

Furious, Jacob ignored the pain in his arthritic knees and stooped to unfasten the bottom bolt. He yanked open the gate and stepped into the narrow lane that ran between the houses and the cliff face.

There was no one there. Whoever it was had either made a swift escape or leapt over a wall into someone else's yard.

"There are CCTV cameras all along this street," he yelled. Not entirely true. Some of the houses had them, but his and Andy's were two of the ones that didn't.

"Whoever you are, you're being filmed, so bugger off before I call the police."

He waited, listened for sounds of anyone moving around or shuffling over one of the walls.

Patches nudged his legs and gazed up at him with enquiring eyes.

"I think they've gone now," he said to the cat. "Fancy the cheek of it, trying to break into your house. C'mon. Let's go back inside."

Dean crept along the front of the terrace, leaping over the low fences until he reached Andy's house. He peered into the window.

The interior was open-plan with a living room leading into the kitchen.

He saw the open back door. The old man was still in the yard.

Dean moved to the front door and tried the handle. *Locked.*

The old guy was a lot smarter than Andy was.

Dean had spotted the security cameras on a couple of the other houses and had managed to keep below their frame. But if the old man had stepped into the back alley, he'd have been forced to reveal himself. Too risky.

The best course would be to take him inside the house where there was no coverage.

He didn't want to risk breaking a window to get in. It could alert one of the other neighbours.

He'd have to wait until the old guy was ready to leave. When he opened the door, Dean would rush him and bundle him back inside.

He grinned, already anticipating the thrill of his knife tearing the old man and the cat apart. His previous killings had all been detached, easily done. He couldn't wait to get up close, to feel with his own hands and see the fear and dread in the old guy's eyes before his life seeped away.

There was movement and sound from behind the door. He was coming.

Dean silently drew his blade.

Then there were other sounds. Laugher, followed by a dog bark.

There were people farther up the bank, coming around the bend. They would be here in mere moments.

He waited, tense, for the door to be unlocked.

What the fuck is the old cunt doing in there?

The voices were louder, closer.

Fuck.

Dean sprinted across the garden, leapt the wall and hurried down the road away from the house. He stuffed the knife into his backpack.

He had missed his moment.

For a few seconds, rage threatened to overwhelm him. With incredible willpower he brought it under control.

So what if the old man lived. He was not the real target. He'd been an opportunity, nothing more – and he had missed it.

Dean had been unprepared. It wouldn't happen again.

For his next move, nothing would go wrong.

Chapter Eighteen

Andy was in his office on Wednesday, wondering what to have for lunch, when his phone rang. It was Jerico.

"Hi." It was impossible not to smile as he answered. Jerico made him giddier now than he had in the old days. Andy felt like he was reliving his youth, only a hundred times better.

"Hey. Got a few minutes?"

"For you? You know I do."

"Good, cause I'm downstairs."

"Eh?"

"Downstairs...in your bar. You told me yesterday how average your coffee is over here, so I thought I'd find out for myself."

He snorted. "I never said that."

"I think you'll find you did," Jerico teased. "So, what do you say? Are you going to come down and treat me...or what?"

Andy set the lock screen on his computer and hurried down, excited to see him again, though it had been less than six hours since they'd been together last. After so many years apart, it was like they were on some mad frenzy to make up for lost time.

Jerico was lounging on one of the leather sofas in the bar, his legs stretched out before him while he flicked through the screen on his phone. He looked up as he sensed Andy's approach and put the phone down. "Hey." He grinned. "Would it be inappropriate if I kissed the boss in here?"

Andy leaned in and planted a kiss on his upturned mouth. "Not if he kisses you first." He slipped into the armchair opposite the sofa. "Anyone would think you had all the time in the world, that you didn't have a new business launching on Friday."

"I needed a break. I also thought you might be ready for lunch, and I didn't want you wandering the streets on your own again." Jerico winked.

"Ah, so that's it. You don't trust me."

"Can you blame me? Got your alarm on you?"

Andy patted his trouser pockets. They were empty. "Shit. Must have left it on my desk."

Jerico's eyebrows rose. "You see? That's why I worry about you."

"Well, I'm glad you're here, whatever suspicious reasons you have."

Roda came over from the bar to take their order.

"Are you eating?" Andy asked.

Jerico groaned and rubbed his belly. "Just coffee for me, please. I've been tasting food all morning. I think I might bust a gut if I eat another mouthful."

Andy asked for two coffees and a tuna melt for himself.

"What's Patches having for lunch today?" Jerico asked. "Smoked salmon? Fillet steak?"

"I left him with a big bowl of biscuits this morning. It should keep him going until I get home. I don't intend to be late tonight. If he's hungry, he can go out and catch his own lunch."

"Mmm. Hot mouse. I think Patches is used to something far more refined than vermin."

Andy loved his goofiness. It reminded him of the younger version so much. "What's put you in such a good mood? I take it everything is going well."

"I'll probably kick myself for saying this, but it's going better than I could ever have imagined. We could open tonight if we wanted to. We're that on top of things."

"Aah, that's such good news. This time last week, you would never have thought that was possible."

He grimaced. "Too bloody true. I also had a call from the police this morning."

"Good news?"

He shook his hands. "Yes and no. They still haven't traced Dean, but they think there might have been a sighting of him in Durham."

"That's where he used to live, right?"

"It is. It means nothing, though. Even if it was him — and they can't confirm that — it's hardly the end of the Earth. Ninety minutes down the motorway, tops. He could come and go as he pleases between Nyemouth and Durham. It used to take me longer than that to get to work each day when I lived in London."

Jerico furrowed his brow. Andy hated to see him like this. The biggest event of his career was about to take place, and a cloud of fear and uncertainty hung over the entire venture. Some jealous little shit with an inferiority complex was going to spoil everything. "The police will be there on Friday night, right?"

"Maybe. They say they can't guarantee it at this moment, not unless Dean attempts something else between now and then."

"That's shit," Andy growled. "I'm so sorry. At least you've got Richie and his team. They'll be more use to you than the cops would be anyway."

Jerico sighed. "I know you're right. Anyway, I came over here to see you, not let that bastard take up more of my time."

Roda returned with their coffees. She set down the cups and saucers and a bowl of sugar sachets and a small jug of cream. "Food won't be long," she said, leaving them again.

Jerico emptied two brown sugars into his cup and a good splash of cream. He brought the cup to his lips and sipped. "Mmm," he said, rolling his eyes. "You were right. That's the most mediocre coffee I've ever tasted."

They both exploded in hysterics.

With everything going on right now, it did feel good to laugh.

From the reception area, Dean Ferguson watched Jerico and Andy in the hotel bar, looking very fucking cosy. *Keep laughing, you sad bastard. Your whole world is about to end.*

Neither of them would have recognised him. Dean had changed his appearance again. Raised shoes had added an inch and a half to his height. He wore a baggy grey suit from a charity shop, padded underneath to create a false beer belly and huge arse. Cotton wool balls puffed out his cheeks and altered the shape of his face. Clear-lensed, tortoise-shell glasses and a reddish-blond wig completed the transformation. The wig looked exactly what it was, cheap and fake, but to any observer, he would be a dreary little man trying to conceal his baldness rather than Jerico's number one stalker.

Jerico and Andy were so caught up in each other that he could walk through the bar right now, and they wouldn't notice. Let them wallow in their ignorance. They'd know who he was when he was ready.

He checked into the hotel using a false ID and a prepaid credit card. He spoke to the receptionist with a strong Scottish accent — another skill he had learned in prison, the ability to mimic accents. He'd spent years building up the weapons in his armoury, waiting for a day like this.

"Are you here on holiday?" the receptionist enquired, professional and friendly.

"Just passing through on my way home," he said, pleased at how well the accent came off. "I looked online last night and saw you had a vacancy. Thought I might as well treat myself."

"Oh, yes, you've been incredibly lucky. We're fully booked for weeks, but we still get the odd cancellation."

He'd passed the hotel plenty of times while he'd been getting a feel for the town, but this was the first time he'd been inside. It was okay, typically old-fashioned with a few modern twists to appeal to a younger traveller. There were hotels just like it up and down the coast, but Dean wasn't here for the facilities or to leave a favourable review.

He accepted the key card and took the elevator to the third floor, careful to use his knuckle on the control panel and not leave any prints. He took his time wandering along the corridor, noting the position of the staircases and fire exits. His room was on the back of the building, facing the street that ran along the rear. It was smart enough but lacking in natural light. He opened all the curtains wide and turned on the main lights.

There was no plan. Dean had been speaking the truth when he'd told the receptionist he had only booked the room the night before. He'd set up an alert on his phone to let him know when there was a vacancy in Quay House. Yesterday was the first time in a week that it had gone off. All he wanted was to get close to Jerico's boyfriend.

Dean stripped down to his underwear, removing the layers of padding and the stale suit that had formed his disguise. There was a change of clothing in his overnight bag. He put on dark jeans, a plan black T-shirt and black trainers with a navy hoodie. No need for any further disguise. When Andy Quinn looked into his eyes, Dean wanted him to know exactly who he was.

He methodically repacked his case before putting on rubber gloves and wiping down all the surfaces he had touched with disposable sanitising wipes. By now, he was certain the police would be on to him, and Jerico must surely know he was in town, but Dean wasn't going to make their jobs easy. He'd evaded capture for long enough and intended to continue doing so.

When the room was immaculate and all his gear was repacked, he picked up the phone and dialled reception.

"Hello," he said, adopting the thick Scottish accent which was becoming more and more natural. Maybe he would fuck off north of the border, once all this was over. "I'm afraid I've got a problem with my room."

* * * *

"Can you spare a few minutes?"

Andy groaned and checked his watch. "I'm about to go home."

Sheila, the deputy manager, gave an apologetic grimace.

"We've got a guest in three-o-six complaining about his room."

"So? You don't need me for that."

"I've already been up there twice. There's no reasoning with him. He's insisting he speaks to the manager."

Andy's heart sank. "Just tell him I'm not here. You're the deputy. You can handle his complaints as well as I can. What's his problem, anyway?"

"The room's too hot. There's not enough natural light. The bed is too hard. He found dust in a corner."

"Like shit he did." Andy had heard all these complaints before, and they were always crap. The hotel might struggle to recruit staff, but housekeeping was one area they did not cut corners. The cleanliness of the rooms was beyond doubt. While it was true the rooms on the back of the hotel were lacking in light, it was reflected in their price, together with the extra lamps provided. "So, what's the real problem? Is he looking for a complimentary stay with food and drink in exchange for a favourable online review? Cause that's not happening?"

Sheila looked exasperated. "That's just it. He hasn't asked for any freebies yet or threatened a bad rating. I even offered a free bottle of wine to smooth things over. He's just found one thing after another to complain about. I'm starting to think he's an inspector rather than a chancer. I know you want to go, but just in case he is a hotel inspector or a travel reviewer, it might not be a bad idea to go up there. A few minutes with the boss might be all it takes to cool him down."

Andy struggled to hide his irritation. It had been a long couple of days, and Sheila was experienced enough to handle this on her own. "All right," he said, chucking his car keys onto his desk. "Five minutes and that's all. If I smell a hint of bullshit, he's all yours."

She looked relieved. "I think he's just an awkward prick. Want me to come up with you?"

"No, check on the restaurant. If there's anything I need you to follow up on, I'll call."

He didn't trust himself to be civil with her all the way up to floor three. Sheila was a great deputy ninety-five percent of the time, then she'd have days like this, when she couldn't handle the simplest situation. Pain-in-the-arse guests were a part of the hotel trade. Everyone in the business had to be adept at dealing with them, from the bottom to the top.

Andy rebuked himself as he made his way to the lifts. He was hot, tired and stressed. He wanted to get home, take off this fucking suit and enjoy a long, cool shower. He shouldn't take it out on his staff. They'd all been working extra for weeks, and the summer was far from over. He'd have to cut Sheila some slack. It wasn't worth pissing her off for the sake of a discontented guest.

He was already thinking about Patches and a cool beer in the garden when he reached room three-o-six.

The door was answered by a pleasant-looking man in his mid-thirties…not what he'd expected. He'd had the image of an ageing executive in mind when Sheila told him about the complaint.

"Hello…Andy Quinn," he introduced himself in a breezy manner. "I'm the general manager. I understand you have some issues with your room."

The man didn't reply and did not smile. He held the door wide and stepped aside. Andy entered, casting a critical eye over the room. It all looked in order. The bed was made up immaculately. The guest had turned on all the lamps to get as much light as he could in the room. The temperature was comfortable, too, so nothing wrong with the air conditioning.

Andy turned, and the man closed the door.

"What seems to be the problem —"

The expression on the man's face sent a chill right through him. It took less than a second for his brain to make the connection between the hotel guest and the man who had attacked him the other day.

Dean Ferguson.

Dean's hand came from behind his back, revealing the lethal edge of a serrated hunting knife.

Fuck. After all Jerico's warnings, how could he have walked into this?

Chapter Nineteen

Andy should have recognised Dean straight away. He'd studied his photographs and old videos enough times in the last few days. Sure, the images were old. While Dean retained a vestige of the baby-faced hopeful who had competed against Jerico in *Top Cook*, there was something hard-bitten about his features now. Deep wrinkles cut into the flesh around his dark eyes. A jagged scar ran from the right corner of his mouth, all the way down his chin. And yet, as soon as Andy had looked twice, he'd seen him for what he was. In many ways he hadn't changed at all.

He was short, no more than five-six or seven, and held himself with the try-hard arrogance of a man attempting to compensate for what he lacked. His body language was tight, coiled like a snake preparing to strike.

"Dean," Andy said, backing into the room. He'd made a fatal blunder coming inside. Apart from the windows, there was no other way in or out, and a jump from the third floor would be disastrous. The only defence available was to reason with the madman.

"You know who I am, then?" His voice was surprisingly soft with a northern accent. Durham or Middlesbrough, something from that area.

"Sure, I do. I've seen you on TV. I'm a fan."

"Bollocks." His voice hardened. "No one remembers me for being anything other than Jerico's crazy stalker."

"And why is that?" Andy was determined not to show fear. *Treat him like a dangerous animal. Don't let him think he's in charge.*

"Because your boyfriend made sure everyone saw me like that—a sour failure, the nutcase who couldn't bear to lose."

"You mean Jerico?"

"Who else?" When Dean sneered, he revealed the full extent of the scar on his face. It was nasty, too ragged to have been caused by a knife. It looked more like a glass or bottle wound. Whoever had done that to him had shown no mercy.

Andy needed to get into that mindset, except there were no glasses in the bedroom, only coffee cups. The nearest glass was in the bathroom. He could make a run for it, but he knew the locks were insufficient. Three years ago, they'd had trouble breaking into a room for a guest who had suffered a heart attack, and all the bathroom locks had been replaced by ones that could be opened from the outside in an emergency. All that was needed was a coin to turn the catch.

Or a blade.

"Don't try to pretend he's not your boyfriend," Dean continued, taking two steps nearer. "I've been watching you…both of you, the nights he spends at your house. The two of you together in the bar this afternoon."

Shit. Jerico had been right to be worried. Andy had written his concerns off as excessive, but Jerico had known the threat they were facing far better than he did.

"The spirit you threw in my eyes."

A smile twitched at the corners of his mouth. "You thought it was acid. Easily done, wasn't it? Just imagine the damage I could have done if I'd wanted to."

"Why did you do it?"

Dean waved the knife and took another step towards him. "To scare you. To prove what I can do."

"You've certainly proven that."

Dean grinned, exposing small, yellowed teeth. "I've done enough scaring. I'm ready to take it up a notch, to let your boyfriend see exactly what I'm capable of."

He advanced farther and reached the bottom of the double bed, edging Andy closer to the window. Andy was fast running out of options. Dean slashed the blade towards him with a twisted grin, and Andy felt the rush of air as it cut past.

If he didn't act now, he was finished.

Andy grabbed the back of the dressing table chair. Acting with strength and speed he didn't know he possessed, he swung the chair towards his assailant. He missed, but the surprise caused Dean to step back. Andy seized the advantage and rushed forward. He swung again. Dean twisted away from him, but the chair came down on his shoulder. Andy wished he'd could have mustered more force behind the strike, but it did the job. The knife fell onto the bed.

Andy dropped the chair and ran for the door. It was locked. He fumbled for the catch.

He heard Dean bounce up on the bed behind him, then his feet were on the floor, racing towards him.

The lock clicked open. As Andy slithered through, he saw Dean was almost upon him. In the corridor, he yanked the door shut. Dean thudded against the other side. Andy tore along the hall. His only chance was to put as much distance as possible between them.

He heard the door open again and Dean's swift tread upon the carpet, chasing him.

He might be short, but he was swift.

If he could get that knife in Andy's back, it would be over.

Summoning an even greater burst of speed, he raced for the end of the hall. His hand dug into his trouser pocket, retrieving his master pass key.

There was a bedroom ahead.

The passkeys could be temperamental and take several swipes before they worked. He prayed it would function the first time.

He reached the door and swiped the card. The light on the panel turned green.

Andy shoved into the room, but Dean was right behind him, the knife raised. Andy put his weight against the door, but before the lock could click shut, Dean's collided against the other side.

Andy dug his feet into the floor, shoving his shoulder against the wood, forcing it. Dean was surprisingly strong and managed to hold his advantage.

Yelling through gritted teeth, Andy gave it everything he had. The door moved a centimetre, then another. Dean continued to push back. Andy thought he would never win, until with a final surge of strength, he felt the door shut and the lock engage.

Dean roared in rage and pounded on the other side.

Andy didn't hesitate. He raced across the room for the phone. There were no security staff on duty. This evening there wasn't even a concierge. He dialled straight down to reception.

"Police," he yelled when someone picked up. "Get the police *now*. There's a man with a knife on the premises."

* * * *

Andy swallowed a glass of whisky in two sudden gulps. It burned his throat and lit a fire in his stomach but did little to ease his tension. He leaned against the side of his desk, too agitated to sit, and took deep breaths. He'd heard it helped to count to five on each inhale and exhale, but his attention faltered on the count of three.

Sheila splashed another generous shot of whisky into the glass and rubbed his shoulder.

Quay House was crawling with police officers. That was terrible for business and they would certainly unsettle the guests, but he couldn't focus on that right now. Damage limitation was a problem for tomorrow — and maybe someone other than him.

DC Andrea Brown came through the open door. "CCTV cameras have got him going down the back stairs and out through the rear fire exit. We've got officers out there now checking the security cameras of neighbouring properties. He appears to have headed in the direction of Bridge Street, towards the bus station."

"You won't find him," Andy said. Dean Ferguson had outwitted the police and evaded capture for weeks. He wouldn't make a mistake now, not when he was so close to achieving his objectives.

"We'll get him," the Detective Constable said.

"He walked through our door wearing a complete disguise. He wore gloves to avoid leaving prints in the room, and he went back to collect his stuff before legging it. He knows what he's doing. Wherever he went, he'll have had another change of clothes and a means of escape."

"I don't think he's that clever," DC Brown said. "If he was, he wouldn't have come here in the first place."

"He's fucking with us. The petrol bomb, the fake acid attack, coming here today... He's letting Jerico know that he's in Nyemouth and he can do anything he wants, anytime he wants to." He took another drink of whisky, slower this time. Poor Jerico. He'd had to endure ten years of harassment. Dean had only been in Andy's life for a few days, and he'd already sacred the shit out of him. How had Jerico managed to endure it for so long?

"It's frightening, I know. But we'll catch him. He's getting sloppy, and sloppy people make mistakes."

Her words did not encourage him. There was nothing to back them up.

They were interrupted by a commotion in the corridor outside.

"You can't go in there," a voice said.

Then Jerico. "Let me through. I need to see him."

Andy rushed across the office and into the hall. Two uniformed police officers were attempting to turn Jerico away.

"Let him through," he shouted.

Then Jerico was racing towards him, and his arms were open. They threw themselves at each other. Andy clung to him, and buried his face into Jerico's neck as emotion overwhelmed him. Tears sprung from Andy's eyes.

"Oh my God, are you okay?" Jerico hugged him tight. "If that bastard has hurt you, I'll kill him. No more fucking courts or police, I'll deal with him own my own."

Andy hugged him even tighter. "I'm fine. He didn't catch me."

"He could have done anything to you. He's crazy. I'm so sorry, Andy. I've brought all this madness into your life. I never would have come here if I'd known the risks involved."

Andy sniffed. The power of Jerico's hold, the reassuring warmth of his body, had a calming effect. "You didn't do anything. Dean's the one who chose this course of action."

"I underestimated him. I should have known he'd follow me."

Andy shook his head. "He's the one to blame for all this. No one else."

They went back into the office. Andy poured Jerico a whisky, and they sat together on the sofa in the corner. Jerico took his hand and held it softly in his own. Though he'd been through it all with the police, Andy told the story again for Jerico's benefit. "He was here this afternoon, when we were in the bar. He saw us."

"Shit. He could be anywhere, and we'd never know until he was right beside us. I'm not taking any more risks," Jerico said. "I'm leaving town. I'm the one he wants, so he can follow me and leave you alone."

"No."

"I have to keep you safe." Jerico heaved a sad, exasperated sigh.

"You can't give him what he wants. That's how he wins, and we can't let that happen."

"Rafiq can open the restaurant without me."

Andy squeezed his hand. "It's your dream. You can't give up on it."

"It's Wednesday now," Sheila said, in a practical tone. "They might pick the fucker up tonight or tomorrow?"

"And they might not," Jerico said.

"You've already arranged security," Andy told him. "They'll keep you and the business safe, at least for the first weekend. You can go to ground next week, if you still want to, but don't let him take your dream away from you."

Jerico twisted on the sofa, looking at him directly. "*You're* my dream. The restaurant is just a business."

"It's *your* business, and it's important. If you quit now, he's won. Don't give the bastard the satisfaction."

"What about you? Can you leave town until they catch him? You could go somewhere safe. You must know plenty of other hotel managers who can put you up. I'll join you after the weekend."

Andy had found his resolve. His encounter with Dean had shaken him, left him unsettled in the aftermath, but his moment of weakness was over. "I'm staying. Nyemouth is *my* town and he's not going to frighten me off. My home is here—my family, my cat, my job and now you. I'll be there on opening night, at the table you promised, with all my friends. I'll be there to give you my support and show Dean fucking Ferguson that a sad little man like him will *never* get in the way of our happiness."

Chapter Twenty

"Look... I can see everything." Andy handed his phone to Jerico. "Swipe through the screens to check out all the cameras."

It was after ten p.m. and the CCTV cameras had switched to night vision, but the image was pristine, taking in the whole of Andy's front garden and part of the road in front. Jerico flicked across and saw another perfect picture of the back yard, followed by the same area from the other side, taking in more of the alley that ran behind the house.

"They also installed security lights front and back," Andy continued, "and the doors and windows are all alarmed."

Jerico scrolled back through the screens and was impressed to find he could zoom in on specific objects with only a minor decrease in picture quality. "They installed all this today?"

"Richie sent a team up while I was at work. They had it done by the time I got back. Pretty efficient, eh."

"Very. You know, you should have had all this stuff before. A single man, living alone, you needed security. I noticed most of your neighbours already have equipment."

Andy laughed softly. "What the hell for? I've got nothing worth stealing. My TV and laptop are both cheapies. I don't have any expensive Rolexes or antiques. And until you came into my life, I've had no experience of homicidal stalkers."

Jerico gave him a playful nudge. "You need to be prepared for anything." Andy was right, though. Jerico had gotten so used to looking over his shoulder and expecting the worst, he'd lost sight of the fact that this wasn't normal for most people. Since he'd crossed paths with Dean Ferguson, security had become a necessity. Wherever he had lived, Jerico had fitted cameras and alarms if they hadn't already been installed. It pained him to think he had brought that kind of paranoia into Andy's previously peaceful world.

Patches jumped onto the bench and trotted over to Jerico to give an affectionate head bump to his hand. Jerico gave Andy his phone back and treated Patches to a gentle rub behind the ear. He responded appreciatively, tilting his head for easier access.

"What about this guy? Won't he trigger the alarms?"

"They are on the doors and windows, not the cat flap," Andy joshed. "I don't think it would matter, anyway. He doesn't go out at night anymore. I can lock the cat flap when I go to bed."

Jerico thought of the damage Dean could cause through that little opening. Squirting a can of petrol through the hole, followed by a couple of lit matches — the ground floor ravaged by flames while Andy slept upstairs. He kept the fear to himself. He'd caused Andy more than enough anxiety. Instead, he said, "Sounds like a good idea."

Andy tapped at the phone and music came through the Bluetooth speakers on the counter. Vintage Elton John. "There's a bottle of wine in the fridge. Pour us a couple, and I'll find us something to eat."

Jerico put his hands on Andy's hips to move around him in the small kitchen, deliberately brushing his groin against Andy's butt as he did so. Andy murmured appreciatively.

The wine was chardonnay with a screw top. Jerico located the glasses and poured two large measures. After another long day at the restaurant, he was ready for a drink and some leisure time.

Andy took out a chopping board and got to work on shallots and mushrooms. "How did Richie get on at the venue?"

Jerico leaned against the counter and watched Andy work. He was so used to cooking for other people, it was nice to relax and do nothing in the kitchen. "It's all looking good. After what happened yesterday, he has increased the number of staff he's bringing in. He seems to have everything covered and thought of things I never would have myself."

"That's his job."

"That's what he said. Told me to forget about security and focus on my own work."

Andy looked at him, his head tilted, and the smile he gave turned Jerico into a warm mush. "He's right. Don't lose sight of that. Tomorrow night your dream will come true. Don't let Dean take the shine off it. He has tainted enough of your career already."

Jerico sipped the wine and sighed. "I wish you'd come back into my life long before now. The tough times wouldn't have been so bad if I'd had you with me."

"I'm here now—and I'll be there tomorrow. We'll get through it together."

Andy made a light meal of creamed mushrooms on toasted sourdough. It was delicious with a hint of wine and melted Emmental cheese. They ate at the small kitchen table. After weeks of planning his perfect menus, Jerico adored the informality of it. Without Andy, he would still be down at the restaurant, working through the night and obsessing over minute details. Now he had a reason to turn off from work and allow himself to relax.

When they had finished, they washed up together before refreshing their glasses and moving through to the living room. They sat on the sofa, facing each other, their legs entwined in the middle. Jerico leaned his arm on the back rest, laid his head against it and gazed adoringly at the most handsome man he'd ever met.

"Tired?" Andy asked.

"Exhausted, but I don't think I'll get much sleep tonight."

"What was it like before? You've had first nights working at other restaurants and being on TV. How did you deal with the nerves then?"

"I don't think I've ever *dealt* with them. Most times, I've managed to use them to my advantage. To be honest, when I was younger, I think I used to get off on the stress. But back then, it was only my reputation at stake. This time it's my reputation and every penny I've ever saved."

"Are you worried?"

"About the restaurant? No. It's everything I wanted it to be, only better. I'm scared about what Dean will do to ruin it...and the people he's prepared to hurt to achieve that."

Andy stretched his hand across the sofa and took hold of Jerico's. "Sshhh. Think about the good things, not that. Remember what Richie told you? Let the professionals do their job and concentrate on your own. You're going to smash it. I know you will. And that little fuckwit will just have to fester in his jealousy when he sees your latest success."

Jerico squeezed his hand and smiled, pretending to share Andy's confidence and hiding the truth well.

By midnight they had finished the wine and were ready for bed. Andy told Jerico to go up ahead of him while he gave Patches his late-night feed and locked up. Jerico went to the front door and tested it.

"Don't you trust me?" Andy sounded bemused as he spooned cat food into a bowl, while Patches yowled urgently at his feet.

"Old habits die hard. This is my routine before I go to bed every night."

When he was satisfied that the back door was also secure, Jerico went upstairs. He now brought a small toilet bag when he stayed over with Andy. He washed his face, gargled and brushed his teeth. While Andy went into the bathroom after him, Jerico stripped to his briefs and looked out of the window. There was no sign of anyone lurking out there, just the dimming lights of the town below and their reflections upon the water.

I would be happy here. This could be the start of the rest of my life. Jerico knew, despite all the good things he had going, he would never settle in Nyemouth until the problem of Dean Ferguson was eliminated. *Where the fuck are you, you bastard?*

"Close the curtains," Andy said, coming into the room behind him. "This place is more secure than a bank tonight. There's nothing to worry about."

Jerico apologised and shut out the world. He watched as Andy removed his shirt and stepped out of his jeans. "The view is much better in here, anyway."

Andy ran his hand across the front of his black boxer-briefs, outlining the hardness inside. "It's pretty fine from where I'm standing, too."

Jerico wriggled his eyebrows and twitched his cock, causing the front of his own underpants to stretch. "I can think of one way it could be better."

"I totally agree."

From across the room, they mirrored each other's actions, hooking their thumbs into their briefs and sliding them down. Andy teased his over his cock, stretching it downwards until his pants came clear, and it sprang back to full mast. They stood completely naked.

"Now, isn't that better?" Jerico said.

Andy went to the bedside table and opened the drawer, giving Jerico a perfect view of his deliciously beefy arse. Andy produced a strip of condoms and a bottle of lube. "I think we'll need these."

At that, Jerico couldn't stop himself. He crossed the room in two steps and grabbed Andy's naked body. They fell onto the bed, their mouths locked in a deep kiss, while they pushed and slid against each other. Their hard, wet cocks created a stickiness on their bellies that drove Jerico crazy with desire. He gripped Andy's butt in both hands and pulled his hips tight against his own.

"Fuck me," Andy pleaded.

Jerico understood his urgency. After all that they'd been through, they had to have each other completely, no time to waste on foreplay or horsing around. The only thing that would satisfy was for one of them to be inside the other.

They shuffled across the bed. Andy rolled onto his back and opened his thighs, raising them high to expose his hole. Jerico stared with undisguised hunger while he stretched a condom over his cock and rolled it to the base. He covered his fingers in lube and ran them through Andy's crack, playing with and stretching his hole before easing inside. Andy moaned, lifting his arse higher. Jerico pushed his fingers deep, thrilled by the heat and tightness of Andy's body. He added more lube, making sure Andy was well prepared before dribbling it over his dick, stroking until the full length glistened.

He climbed above Andy, getting in position. He ran his cock along his butt crack, tracing the rim with his head, before pushing in. Jerico went easy, entering him a slow inch at a time, until he was completely enveloped.

"Oh, that's it." Andy sighed, hooking his ankles around Jerico's waist. "Let me feel it all."

Covering Andy with his body, holding him, loving him, Jerico gave a good long twitch of his cock.

Andy groaned and gripped him tighter. "More."

Jerico complied, pulsing his cock inside Andy's tight hole, planting kisses over his brow and cheeks all the while. Then he started to thrust, easing his hips back and forth, maintaining a gentle pace. Andy raised his head for more kisses. Their breath merged in their mouths.

Jerico kept it going, long and slow for as long as he could manage. "Going have to fuck you," he groaned. "I've got to have you."

"Yes," Andy hissed. "Do it."

Jerico eased back onto his knees. Andy adjusted position beneath him. He straightened his legs and raised them to Jerico's shoulders. Jerico gripped his ankles, kissed his shin, and fucked him with greater passion. The wet, rhythmic crack of skin against skin filled the room.

Andy twisted his head from side to side, arched his neck and begged for more. Jerico rested Andy's ankles on his shoulders and spread his hands across his exposed torso, caressing his chest and nipples, moving down his flanks. Then he seized Andy's hips in both hands and gave it to him with everything he had.

"I can't...last...much longer," Andy gasped.

"Then come," Jerico said, stoking him long and deep.

Andy licked his lips and grabbed his cock. His body tensed as he tugged. He stiffened, then opened his eyes, staring up at Jerico. He opened his mouth as he came, releasing a primal cry of ecstasy, spraying his chest and belly with a hot, milky load. The tightening of his body when he came took Jerico over the edge. He clutched Andy's hips as his cock contracted and released his orgasm with one intense pulse after another.

Afterwards, Jerico disposed of the condom and tissues Andy had used to wipe his stomach, and they snuggled together, with Andy's back pressed against his chest. The night was too warm for covers, and a single sheet shielded their bodies to the waist.

"This time tomorrow, all the worry will be worth it," Andy said. "Your first night will have been a huge success."

"Let's not jinx it in advance," Jerico murmured.

"Don't be so negative. You've got everything covered. For all we know, the police might already have Dean in custody."

Jerico doubted that but didn't want to waste any more energy worrying about the bastard.

Andy yawned. His breathing deepened, and within minutes, he was asleep.

Despite his physical exhaustion, Jerico's mind was busy, working through all the things that could go wrong in the next twenty-four hours, including some he'd never considered until then. He couldn't relax or enjoy everything he'd worked towards, not with such an ominous cloud hanging over him.

Although it was a blessing to lie beside this exceptional man, he knew sleep was some way off.

It was the beginning of a long and lonely night.

Chapter Twenty-One

By six o'clock on Friday evening, Jerico had barely had a spare second all day to worry about Dean Ferguson. He'd been working full out since eight that morning, ensuring everything was perfect. His guests were due to arrive in an hour's time and despite his opening-night nerves, he knew they were in a good place. The fresh food supplies that could only have been delivered today had arrived on time. He had a full quota of staff, both front of house and back.

Every one of them had been searched on their way in by Richie's security team. This had struck Jerico as excessive. He doubted Dean's disguises were so good that he could have secured himself a job there, but after Richie pointed out that they didn't know if Dean was working alone, he hadn't argued. There still seemed little point in searching his staff for concealed weapons when the kitchen was full of knives, but he decided to step aside and let the security staff do their jobs.

Even Rafiq was chilled.

"It's wonderful," his partner said as they carried out their final checks on the dining room.

The tables were set with deep red cloths and napkins, custom made china and cutlery. There were displays of fresh flowers on each table and in every window. Their intended vibe had been traditional with a modern twist, and they had nailed it.

"It's everything we ever talked about," Jerico said proudly.

Rafiq patted him on the back. "Everything and more."

As they reached the bar, Rafiq asked for two glasses of champagne.

"Oh, no," Jerico said. "I need to keep a clear head. I've got a full night of work ahead of me."

Rafiq batted away his objections. "We have to toast and celebrate…for luck, while it's just us. Once those doors open, this will become bigger than you or I."

He had a point. Jerico asked the server to only pour him a third of a glass. His time to celebrate would come later, once the mayhem of service was over.

"Here we are, my friend," Rafiq said, raising his glass. "To Osman's Syrian Kitchen. The first of many. Cheers."

They clinked glasses. "Cheers," Jerico said, "though I'm not ready to think about franchising yet. Let's make a success of this place first."

"It's already a success. Have you seen the booking diary? There are hardly any free tables until the autumn."

"That's one season. We'll be a success if we're still as popular this time next year."

Rafiq rolled his eyes. "Always thinking small. Where is your ambition?"

As Jerico returned to the kitchen, he met Richie coming in the back door. The handsome security officer looked the business in his black uniform, with stab-proof vest and body cam. "Got a minute for a final run-through?"

"Sure. I haven't had time to even thank you for all this. I'm grateful for everything you've done on short notice."

"It's looking good," Richie said. "My team at the front are all ready. Your guests will be bag-searched and wanded down, but don't worry. It will be done in as civil a manner as possible, and everyone will be made to feel welcome."

The idea of body-searching guests at a restaurant filled him with horror, but after what had happened to Andy this week, Jerico had quashed his reservations. Safety had to be the top priority.

"There are guys at the back, and I'll be conducting a perimeter walk around the block throughout the evening. There are police out there, too. Two cars at either end of the block. It's a good position. They are close enough if Ferguson should turn up, but they're not parked directly out the front to ruin your guest's arrival."

Jerico sighed. "I've underestimated Dean before, but surely he's not going to try anything tonight — not when the block is crawling with security and coppers."

"The best security is a deterrent. We don't want anything to happen, but we're prepared if it does. He'd have to be one stupid bastard to even think about trying to do something tonight."

There were a lot of things Jerico could call Dean, but stupid wasn't one of them. He'd managed to avoid capture for over a week. He'd gotten close to Jerico without him even noticing. Dean was fearless, reckless and certainly dangerous, but it would be a massive mistake to dismiss him as stupid.

* * * *

Andy fed Patches before going two doors along to Matt and Jake's place. When he'd invited the guys to his table, they had insisted that everyone begin the evening at their place with cocktails. He'd been unsure what to wear for the event. Jerico had insisted there be no dinner suits or formal wear and that smart casual was as strict a dress code as there would be. It was another warm night, so in the end, he opted for a pair of dark blue linen trousers, a white open-neck shirt and a lighter blue sports jacket.

The guys were already sitting in the front garden when Andy arrived. There was an uncorked bottle of champagne on the table.

"Come on in," Jake said, spotting Andy as he approached the gate.

"You're all looking good," Andy remarked, happy to see the other men had followed Jerico's guide and gone for open-necked shirts and sports jackets.

Jacob shuffled his chair around so Andy could get to the garden table.

Matt poured him a glass of champagne. "I've got a couple of different cocktails ready to go in the kitchen," he said, "but thought we could finish the bubbles first."

"How's it going down there?" Jake asked. "Have you heard from Jerico?"

He shook his head and tasted the champagne. It was delicious. "No. And I didn't want to bother him. I doubt he'll have a minute to look at his phone, anyway."

"He must be a bundle of nerves right now," Jake said. "I remember when me and Lizzie first opened the café. We were manic in the days beforehand. Lizzie is usually the calming influence, but even she was high as a kite. And that's just a local café. We didn't have any of the press or VIP's that will be there tonight."

"He'll be fine," Matt said. "Jerico must be used to the fame and attention by now."

It wasn't the press and social media attention Osman's Syrian Kitchen was about to get that worried Andy. It was an altogether darker interest that troubled him, but he didn't want to spoil the mood by mentioning Dean. He hadn't told his neighbours about the incident at the hotel the other day.

"How's your mam?" Jacob asked. "Is she meeting us there?"

"She took the afternoon off to get her hair and make-up done professionally. She wants to go full glam, so yeah. She's going to text me when she's ready, and I'll meet her at the door."

"Arnie and Dominic will meet us there, too," Jacob said. "I think AJ had something going on at school this afternoon that they couldn't get out of."

"It will be a proper South Bank reunion," Jake said. "I can't remember when we last had a good night out." He looked at his husband, Matt. "Any idea?"

Matt whiffled his lips and ran his fingers through his thick dark hair. "Apart from our weekend away in March, I can't think of anything."

"You work too hard," Jacob says. "You all do."

Jake wriggled his eyebrows. "Says the man who's still the lifeboat treasurer in his mid-seventies."

Jacob grinned. "That's voluntary work. It's not the same."

Andy admired the old man's dedication and grit. He hoped he had half of his stamina once he retired. Jacob had committed his life to the service of the local station, much like Jake was now — and their pal Dominic. Andy didn't know where they found the time. They were all so busy with their professional lives, but when their pagers rang, they answered the call of duty to save anyone in trouble on the sea. They were the lifeblood of the community. When it came around to their fundraising events, the annual summer fayre, the Christmas and Easter raffles, Andy made sure that the hotel contributed a great prize to their cause, but it was nothing compared to what these guys did. They risked their own lives every time they went out on a call.

Would Jerico settle into the community once the restaurant was established? Matt had come to Nyemouth as a tourist, looking for a summer holiday and break. He'd met and fallen in love with Jake and had never left. He'd even opened his own law firm here in town. He wondered if Jerico would ever settle down like that. He'd spent the last twenty years travelling the world in one way or another. Could he ever be happy in a little town like this?

He looked at Jake and Matt, so happy together, so obviously in love and wondered if there was any chance of that being part of his own future.

One thing at a time, Andy. Someone tried to kill you just two days ago. How about focusing on getting through the weekend in one piece before you start planning your happily ever after?

They finished the champagne.

"Let me get those cocktails," Matt said, getting to his feet.

"I'll give you a hand." Andy followed him inside.

The house was identical in layout to his own place, with the open-plan living room and kitchen. The main difference was that it was immaculate. Everything was perfect and nothing out of place. It was obviously a pet-free home. Despite the scratch posts Andy had all over his house, Patches has made claw marks on all his furniture.

Matt took two glass jugs from the cupboard and filled each one with ice.

"What can I help with?" Andy asked.

Matt gestured to two bottles of spirit on the counter. "Half fill one with vodka and the other with gin."

"So, what are we having?"

"The gin is for a Tom Collins, the vodka for a Jackie Collins." Matt rummaged in the fridge, then the freezer, returning to the counter with his hands full. He cut a lemon in half. "Which is gin?"

Andy pushed the jug towards him. Matt squeezed both ends of lemon over the gin and ice mixture until they were dry. Then he cut another into slices and tossed them in. Next he splashed sugar syrup into the jug, before topping it up with soda and giving it a good stir.

"I'm sure most mixologists will be appalled at my methods, but it tastes just as good this way."

To the vodka jug, he added frozen raspberries, more sugar syrup, a good third of raspberry juice and topped it all up with lemonade. Andy carried the jugs to the table while Matt followed him out with four martini glasses.

Andy opted for the raspberry-flavoured Jackie Collins. "Oh my God, this is delicious." He took another hearty drink. "My mam will go bonkers for this stuff. You'll have to tell her how to make it."

"Even better, get her to come over one night, and we'll have a cocktail party. We can put on her songs and dance. It will be great."

"You won't have to ask her twice."

Jacob puckered his lips after tasting the gin cocktail. "Crikey, that's a sharp one."

"You know where we keep the whisky," Jake said, "if you prefer something else."

"This is fine. Just not what I'm used to, that's all. It might take a sip or two to adjust."

They all laughed. It felt so good to unwind like this. Jerico's return to his life had been a surprise, a whirlwind of happiness and heightened emotions, but there was no denying that the last week had also been one of the most stressful periods of his life. He wouldn't have thought it possible to experience such highs and lows, all at the same time. It was like being on a rollercoaster again and again with no way of getting off.

He hoped tonight would be another of those highs.

* * * *

They left the neighbours' house at twenty-past-seven, making their way down the bank towards the restaurant, laughing and smiling like kids on their holidays.

The smiles and the laughter wouldn't last for long.

Dean watched them from the other side of the river. Sitting on the edge of the harbour, with his binoculars trained on South Bank Terrace, he'd seen it all. The four men drinking in the garden, then a flurry of activity as they'd locked the house and made their way to the party.

As they came down the hill, he lost them behind the buildings on Pier Street.

Dean wasn't worried. He knew exactly where they were going.

He'd be heading that way himself in a little while.

His insides churned with excitement. He'd done well to control himself this week. He'd almost lost it on Wednesday. Going after Andy at the hotel had been a mistake. It was just as well he'd fucked up. If he'd succeeded, his plans for tonight might have come to nothing.

This way would be so much better.

Dean stood and threw the binoculars into the river. They bobbed on the surface for a moment or two before sliding under the still water. He'd bought them yesterday at a second-hand store along the coast. Cheap, but effective, they were now of no further use to him. He watched them as they sank. The water was clear, and it surprised him how long it took for them to disappear.

Gone. He would vanish just as efficiently when his work was done.

But not yet. His plan had barely started.

Dean turned away from the river and headed for the steps that led to North Point.

Chapter Twenty-Two

Jerico checked the final platter of food as it came to the kitchen pass.

"Perfect," he said. "*Service please.*"

The tasting platters of mixed starters had gone out to all the tables now. Each one had passed his inspection. With a restaurant filled with critics, foodies, press and VIP's, it was essential that there be no mistakes. His team had surprised themselves.

"Great work, guys," he yelled across the commotion of the kitchen. "But we're just getting started. Don't lose focus now. Twenty minutes until the first main courses go out. Are we going to make it?"

The team answered in unison. "Yes, Chef."

Jerico beamed. There was nothing like the buzz of a busy service. It had been weeks since he'd left his job in Newcastle to devote all his energy to the new business. He'd forgotten how much he loved this aspect of the job.

He wiped his brow on a clean napkin and took a swig of water. He saw a sudden blur as Richie hurried through from the main floor, making his way to the back entrance. He spoke rapidly to the guard on the door. Jerico had been so engaged since the start of service that he'd forgotten all about the risk posed by Dean tonight. He hurried over and tapped Richie on the shoulder.

"What's going on?"

"Nothing we can't handle," Richie said.

Jerico stiffened. "Well, that sounds like *something*."

"Don't worry, just focus on your job."

Jerico gripped his arm. "I'll be able to do that a lot better when I know what the problem is."

After a beat, Richie relaxed into agreement. "We've lost our police attendants."

"How come?"

"It's nothing to be concerned about. There's been an incident up on North Point. They've had to redeploy all officers until they know what's happening." Richie's reassuring tone incited calmness.

"What sort of incident?"

"Some kind of traffic accident. They've had to close the road. It won't impact anything down here. The roads through the town centre are all open, and the police escorts will be back as soon as they are released. In the meantime, I've got more than enough staff on duty to cover us. We didn't need the police, anyway. They were only ever there as a deterrent."

Jerico weighed up the situation. Of course, he couldn't detain the police officers here when they had more serious duties to attend to, and he didn't have the time or the emotional capacity to worry about it. "So, we're all good. Nothing to worry about?"

"Nothing at all. You'll be the first to know if there is. Now go back to what you do. I've seen what it's like in there. Those starter plates didn't touch the sides for most people. You'll have some very hungry guests to worry about if you don't feed them again soon."

Jerico had no choice but to trust him. His role tonight was to run to the kitchen. He had to leave security to the experts.

* * * *

Mari was delighted to be sitting next to Arnie Walker and Dominic Melton and did nothing to hide her joy. Andy chuckled as he watched her from across the table. Mari enjoyed a small-scale level of D-list celebrity, but Arnie Walker was A-list royalty. Though he'd been brought up in Nyemouth and had been living back here for several years, their paths hadn't crossed. Now that they had, she wasn't going to waste an opportunity to mingle with a genuine Hollywood actor.

She raised her phone and pulled Arnie to her side. "Selfie," she shrieked excitedly.

"Mam," Andy protested.

Arnie took it all in good grace and smiled for her camera phone.

"I want photos with everyone," she said. "Jerico will thank me when I post them on my socials and tag this place. It's free publicity."

Andy knew Arnie's husband Dominic from when they used to be neighbours. Before their marriage, Dominic had lived on South Bank Terrace in the house Jake and Matt now owned. He was less familiar with Arnie. They'd met once or twice at social events but had never had the opportunity to become friends. Arnie spent a lot of time working away on location. There was nothing grand or showbizzy about him, however, and he always came across as a down-to-earth and friendly guy whenever they had met.

Tonight was no exception.

"Your mam's right," Arnie said. "We need to tag the hell out of this place. I've taken pictures of everything so far. The food is *so* good."

Andy smiled with pride. He couldn't wait to celebrate Jerico's success with him, but for now, he hadn't even seen him. Jerico was too busy busting his arse in the kitchen to mingle with his guests. It was going brilliantly so far. While everyone at this table was biased, Andy had listened in on conversations from the other diners and heard the food being celebrated all around. There was no shortage of great places to eat in Nyemouth, but Jerico had cannily spotted a gap in the market the local folk hadn't even known they needed.

"That's a marvellous idea," Mari said. She picked a skewer of lamb from the sharing platter and put it on her own plate, raising her phone for another photo.

Andy was feeling pleasantly tipsy. The cocktails Matt had made had set him up for the evening, and they were already onto the third bottle of wine for the table. Jerico had spared no expense, making sure every one of his guests was well catered to with food and drink.

The atmosphere throughout the room was buoyant. None of the guests had been particularly put out by the heightened security on arrival. The process had been efficient and polite, and it had taken no more than twenty or thirty seconds per person. He hoped it had allowed Jerico to relax and focus on his job. It had certainly eased any last-minute nerves Andy might have had. From his two encounters so far, he knew Dean was a wily bastard, but Andy couldn't see there was any way for him to worm his way in here tonight.

"We should book this place for our anniversary," Jake said to Matt as he finished one of the delicious chicken strips.

"I've already looked. We might stand a chance mid-week, but there's no hope of getting in at the weekend. Maybe for your birthday, if we book it now," Matt said.

"You're kidding. It's that popular already?"

"So I've heard," Andy said. "The first available weekend isn't until sometime in the autumn. But hey, I'll always find room for you over at Quay House."

They rolled their eyes in mock horror.

"No offence," Matt said, "but between your place and The Lobster Pot, we've celebrated every special occasion we've ever had together by eating the exact same food."

"None taken," he laughed. "That's exactly why this place is going to be huge. Nyemouth needs more diversity."

As they finished the platter, one of the servers swept in to clear it away and replenish their wine glasses. Andy covered the top of his glass with his hand.

"No, thanks. I need to start pacing myself. I've got to work tomorrow."

"Me, too," Jake said with a grimace. "Though Lizzie is doing the breakfast shift, so at least I don't have to go in early."

"Well, there's nothing stopping us," Mari gushed, beckoning the server to top up hers and Arnie's glasses.

* * * *

Richie Goldman stepped out of the back door of the kitchen. Though it was getting on for nine, it was still balmy after a sweltering day, but nothing compared to the heat inside. He'd never understand how anyone could work in such fierce conditions.

Sophia, one of his best officers, stood guard in the small yard.

"Any news?" he asked her.

"Three seriously injured. There's talk of at least one fatality, but nothing confirmed."

"Shit. That bad?"

"Sounds like it."

Richie hadn't wanted to take the shine off the restaurant opening by telling Jerico about the incident up on North Point. His staff had started to hear news in fractured pieces soon after the police patrols had departed. The cops had confirmed nothing, but it appeared that earlier in the evening a car had crashed into a crowd of people waiting at a bus stop. The rumour now was that the driver had fled the scene — no doubt drunk or high, if that part of the story was to be believed. Whatever the truth, the two patrol cars had made off sharpish, and he had little hope in them coming back before the shift here was over.

Nor would he expect it. They had far more serious matters to deal with.

"How's it going in there?" Sophia asked.

"All good so far."

"Any chance we'll get some leftovers before we go? The smells are making me ravenous."

He laughed. "I'm sure there'll be something to spare. You should see how much food they're cooking. I've never seen so much meat."

"Oh, don't," she groaned, clutching her belly. "You're making it worse."

"Too rich for the likes of us, anyway. I'll treat you all to pizza at the end of the night if there's nothing left to be had here."

"I'll hold you to that."

"Have I ever let you down? I'm going to take a walk around the perimeter. Won't be long."

The back yard led to the alley that divided the restaurant building from a row of shops. Richie went left, turning onto the main road. Having lost their police escorts, he needed to be extra cautious. Jerico's stalker had thrown a petrol bomb through the window just the past week. A similar stunt tonight with a packed crowd inside would be disastrous.

It was still daylight, and there were plenty of people out on the streets—couples and groups dressed up for the night, moving between venues. No one suspicious.

He walked to the end of the building and turned again. The main entrance was situated on the side street that led between the main road and the marina. Two of his guards stood at the front door. A well-to-do middle-aged couple studied the menu on the front of the building.

"He's done well for himself," he heard the woman say to the man as he passed.

Richie hoped Osman's Syrian Kitchen didn't just do well for Jerico but for the town itself. There had been a rise in right-wing ideology in the whole country in recent years, and Nyemouth had been no exception with bigotry and hate crime on the rise. As a black security officer, Richie had put up with more than his share of racism and violence. Jerico's restaurant brought a new flavour of diversity to the town and was another finger in the eye to the Little Britain mentality that had been stoked by right-wing politicians and gutter journalists.

As soon as they had a night off together, he intended to bring Mari for a meal here. They would do their part to support and welcome the new venture.

There was music and raised voices from the direction of the marina, but all was quiet on the street. He turned left again. This side of the restaurant backed onto The Fisherman's Arms pub. It sounded busy enough inside, but the road was quiet.

As he completed the circuit and headed back to the yard, a young man with shaggy blond hair was cutting down from the main street. He stared at his phone as walked, only looking up as their paths crossed.

"Hey," the man said. "Have you seen what's happening on the other side? Up on the point?"

"There's been some kind of incident," Richie said, stepping aside to let the man pass.

"You can say that again."

Richie realised too late that the blond hair was a bad wig, and he failed to react in time.

The man drew a gun from behind his back and shot Richie in the chest.

* * * *

"It's time you made a speech," Rafiq said.

Jerico grabbed a bottle of water and guzzled it down. He wiped his brow on his sleeve. They had reached the end of service for the main courses. They'd agreed he would say a few words to the guests before the desserts were sent out. He checked his watch. *Where had the last few hours gone?*

"All right. Give me a couple of minutes." He took off his sodden chef's tunic and wiped his chest and neck with a clean tea towel. "What's the word out there?"

"Are you kidding? They love it." Rafiq's face glowed. "Did you see a single item of food brought back to the kitchen? Because I didn't. They've eaten everything. They love it."

Jerico enjoyed a small buzz of happiness. He would not relax and enjoy it fully until the end of the night, when the last dish had been served. And even then, he'd be back tomorrow to do it all over again for the people who really counted – the paying customers.

He put on a fresh white tunic. "All right, let's do this." He raised his voice so everyone in the kitchen could hear. "Guys, you've done a great job so far. Follow me out in a few minutes so all those people can see the talented chefs who cooked the best dinner they've ever had."

Jerico followed Rafiq into the dining room. A cheer went up immediately, and as more people realised he was there, it turned into a rapturous applause. By the time he stepped up onto the raised area in front of the bar, most of the guests were on their feet, clapping and cheering.

Bloody hell. It was overwhelming. He'd envisaged a moment like this for over a decade. He'd achieved the kind of career highlights most people could only dream of – winning a TV cookery show, learning his craft in the best Michelin-starred restaurants in the country, cooking private dinners for royalty – but none of it compared to this moment, to stand in the restaurant he'd worked so hard for and be rewarded by this kind of reception.

His gaze moved across the crowd to the table in the right corner. He had a direct eyeline to Andy, who was also on his feet, grinning from ear to ear. Andy gave him two thumbs up before mouthing, "I love you."

Jerico's heart swelled, and his eyes brimmed with tears. "I love you, too," he mimed back and blew a kiss.

Rafiq was speaking, but he couldn't understand a word, then realised Rafiq was queuing him up for his own speech. Words tumbled from his mouth, but he didn't really know what he was saying, either. He thanked everyone for coming, for supporting his new venture. He thanked everyone who had worked with him along the way to make his dream a reality.

"Sorry," he said, taking a breath to gather himself. "I'm rambling, I know. I'm overwhelmed. Instead of listening to me prattle on, why don't you thank the fantastic kitchen team who have worked so hard to make this night possible?"

He relaxed slightly as his staff filed through from the kitchen. The crowd went even wilder, cheering and applauding.

Wow. He wished his mind was more focused, less overwhelmed. He wanted to be able to remember this night forever.

Rafiq raised his hands, bringing the celebrations under control. He had realised Jerico's state and took over again, naming each of the team in turn so they could be acknowledged.

As the excitement began to settle, the celebrations were cut short by the shocking crack of a gunshot.

In an instant, Jerico knew that his greatest fear had been realised.

Dean Ferguson walked out of the kitchen with a gun in his hand and hatred in his eyes.

Chapter Twenty-Three

"The party's over, you greedy fuckers." Dean swaggered into the restaurant. His eyes were so wide they showed the whites all around his irises.

He'd changed very little in the years since Jerico had last seen him, the day the Crown Court judge had sent him to prison. There was a scar on his lower jaw, and an overall hardness to his features that hadn't been there before, but he was essentially the same—small and wiry with short dark hair and a baby-faced aspect. How the hell had he gone around town for over a week undetected?

"I want everyone's hands on the tables where I can see them. Anyone who doesn't comply gets a bullet."

The guests looked at each other in astonishment. Many did what he asked while others thought it some kind of joke, a twisted theatrical stunt for opening night.

"This is all for show, right?" Hannie Wallen was a food critic for *Northeast Life*. Her expression fell somewhere between confusion and fury.

"Do you want to find out the hard way?" Dean's voice cracked.

Jerico had never seen him this unstable. "It's no show," he said. "Everyone, please just do as he says."

The gun swung in his direction. "Don't open your fucking mouth until I'm ready to speak to you." Then back to the guests. "On the table. *Now.*"

They did what he asked. *Thank God.* Jerico cast a glance in Andy's direction. Everyone at his table had done the same. *Stay calm. Please don't draw attention to yourself.* Andy had been Dean's target twice this week and had survived. He might not be so lucky a third time.

With all the guests in compliance, Dean turned his attention to the kitchen staff. "Get on the floor, the lot of you. Hands behind your heads."

No one argued. They all dropped to their knees.

"Not you, twat," Dean snarled at Jerico. "Stay as you are."

There was no sign of any of the security team. Surely those at the front were aware of what was happening and had raised the alarm. Dean had obviously come in the back way. He must have taken down the staff positioned out there. Their best hope of survival was to stall him until the police arrived. If the team out front had called in an alert of a gunman, it wouldn't take them long to get here.

"Anything you say." Jerico kept his tone gentle and compliant.

"Shut the fuck up. I'm not going to tell you again." Dean's voice was high-pitched, cracking once more on the last word. Seemingly satisfied of his secure position, he paced back and forward, keeping the crowd and Jerico in his sights. He chewed his bottom lip.

Jerico's mind raced. How had it come to this? They'd covered every exit. There was no way he should have gotten near the restaurant, let alone through the kitchen. And where had he obtained a gun from? He'd always known Dean was unstable, but this took it to another level. He seemed highly agitated too. *Drugs? Possibly.* Had his time in prison made him worse? Introduced him to criminal influences and given him the contacts he needed to procure a weapon like that?

"Enjoy your dinners, did you?" Dean spoke directly to the people on the nearest table. "*Did you?*"

A woman flinched and burst into tears. Her partner raised his arm to comfort her.

"*Hands down,*" Dean screamed. "I won't tell you again. Keep them on the table unless you want to lose them."

The man did what he was told. The woman dropped her chin to her chest and cried openly.

"Did. You. Enjoy. Your. Dinner?" Dean waggled the gun at the crying woman.

"Yes," she sobbed.

"What was so good about it?"

Her chest heaved as she tried to speak. Jerico tensed with rage. If he was in reach of Dean now, he would go for his throat and throttle the life out of him. *Damn the consequences.*

"It…was…nice…" the woman managed.

"Nice? *Nice?* Is there something wrong with you? Eating this foreign shit. Are you serious? It's stunk out the whole town. I could smell it from the other side of the fucking river. You'll all be fighting over the toilets later when it's exploding out of both ends." He swung the gun back towards Jerico. "The slop they served up in jail is better than anything this fraud cooks."

"Where are the police?" Andy muttered through gritted teeth.

Jake, to his right, gave a tiny shake of his head. "Can't even hear any sirens."

They were far enough from the front to whisper without being heard.

"They should be here by now. They were right outside when we arrived," Andy said.

"I think I can reach my phone," Arnie said. From where he sat, he had his broad back to the front of the room, where Dean continued to rant. "Do you think he can see me from up there?"

Jacob sat directly across from Arnie. "I don't think so," he said. "The next table should block his eyeline."

"Be careful," Dominic urged his husband. "Do it slowly. No sudden movements."

"It's not worth the risk," Mari said. "The police will already be on their way. The guards on the door made it out when he first came in. They'll have called for help."

"Then where are they?" Andy hated how helpless he was. Jerico was caught up in Dean's craziness at the front, and there was nothing he could do about it from here. "Is the gun even real? When he came at me the other day, he pretended it was an acid attack, but all he used was vodka. The gun could be fake, too. We could all rush him."

"No," Mari whispered.

"It's real," Dominic said grimly. "I saw when it went off. If you look up, there's damage to the ceiling. We'll never reach him before he shoots us first."

Andy's breath hissed through his teeth. If that bastard did anything to Jerico, he'd regret the day he was ever born. Andy would rip him to pieces with his bare hands.

Jerico stood beside the bar with his hands on his head. His skin was ashen. *Poor man.* His dream had become a nightmare. All his hard work for nothing. His petty stalker had ruined everything he'd fought so hard to achieve.

"Who the hell is this guy?" Arnie asked.

"Dean Ferguson," Jake said. "Total fuck up. He's been on Jerico's case since he lost out to him on *Top Cook.*"

"That's what this is about?" Dominic snarled. "Some loser from a reality TV show holding a grudge?"

Andy nodded grimly.

"Fuck."

"No heroics," Matt warned. "Let him have his rant then the police will deal with him."

"If he doesn't kill Jerico first," Andy said. He clenched his knuckles, feeling more useless than ever. His heart was somewhere in his throat. It was getting harder to breathe.

"This should be mine," Dean ranted, raking his free hand through his crop of hair.

"Jesus," Dominic muttered. "He's deranged."

"Maybe we can talk about it," a new voice spoke.

Andy strained his neck. It was Rafiq. He could just make out the top of his head.

"I'm Jerico's business partner. I have other restaurant interests. I'm always looking for new opportunities…new talent to invest in."

Good. Humour his delusions. Keep him distracted.

Dean stopped pacing. "You… You paid for this? Not him."

"We're partners," Rafiq said, gaining confidence. "We can discuss your plans, too. What kind of food place are you interested in? Cafés, street food, restaurants. There are so many possibilities."

The room became silent. Rafiq had caught Dean off guard.

Dean looked at him, seeming to struggle with what he had said. "You nurture talent?"

"That's right." Rafiq drew breath. "If…if you let these people go, then we can talk about it. Discuss your plans."

Dean grinned. "You're full of shit. You know nothing about talent. You wouldn't have put your money into this dump and *him* if you did."

"I…didn't know about you, then," Rafiq continued. "I'm serious. Let's talk."

Come on, come on, you stupid prick. Fall for it.

"Didn't know?" Dean nodded. "I guess you didn't. No one knew…because of him." He glared at Jerico, held his gaze, licked his lips. "But now everyone will know."

He swivelled the gun and shot Rafiq in the head.

Jerico let out a cry of pure agony as his best friend crashed backwards against the bar, his limbs splayed at awkward angles. His ears throbbed with the noise from the gun blast. All around he saw faces stricken with terror.

"Shut up," Dean yelled. His voice was pitched so high and loud he was on the verge of losing it. "Shut up or another one of you will get it."

The kitchen team cowered lower to the floor in terror. Many people were crying.

Jerico wanted to tell himself this wasn't happening, that he'd wake from the nightmare in another second. But the grim truth was clear in the spreading pool of Rafiq's blood that seeped across the floor.

Rafiq had a large family — a wife and three children, parents, brothers, sisters. It was a small relief to know none of them had made the journey north for the opening of his latest venture. No loved one should have to witness what had just happened.

Despite Dean's screaming and gesticulating with the gun, he'd lost control of the room. The cold-blooded murder had tipped many of the guests into hysteria. People cried and clung to each other while the madman yelled at them.

Dean stormed up to Jerico. "Make them shut up."

"I can't. They won't. Not after what you've done."

"Shall I shoot more of them? Is that what you want? More innocent blood on your hands."

"This is between me and you. No one else. Let all these people go."

Rage filled Dean's eyes. His mouth twisted in a savage grimace. "It's your fault that I have to do this."

"It's you, Dean. This is all on *you*...every terrible decision you have ever made."

His expression changed again. He giggled. "You think you're so fucking smart."

Dean snatched a linen napkin from one of the dining tables. He hurried to the bar, keeping the gun trained on Jerico. Jerico wouldn't even mind if he just shot him and got it over with. If it would save Andy and everyone else here, he'd accept it willingly.

Dean grabbed a full bottle of brandy from beneath the bar and twisted off the cap. Jerico realised with horror what he was about to do. He lunged towards him, but the bar prevented him from getting hold. Dean stuffed the napkin into the open neck of the bottle and struck a lighter. When the cloth was well lit, he flung it over-arm into the dining room.

By a miracle, it missed a man's head by a hair's width before shattering on the floor. The alcohol ignited in an instant whoosh, and the flames caught onto a tablecloth, setting that alight, too. The guests were in full panic. They ignored Dean's orders to stay still, screaming and rushing for the exits.

Dean was in front of the bar again, he jabbed the muzzle of the gun into the small of Jerico's back. "Through the kitchen," he said. "We're leaving."

It was chaos as smoke filled the room.

Jerico prayed Andy had made it out of the front.

As they reached the kitchen door, he heard his name.

"Jerico." Andy was standing on a chair, scanning the crowd for him.

"Get out," Jerico yelled. "Go, *now*."

Dean spun behind him, and the gun went off again.

Jerico saw a burst of blood on Andy's shirt before he dropped, lost in the smoke and turmoil.

Chapter Twenty-Four

Andy hit the floor hard. Pain cracked through his coccyx and up his back, and for a few seconds it obliterated the agony in his right shoulder…but not for long. He rolled onto his left side and gasped for breath. *He shot me. He actually shot me.*

Someone's foot caught him in the lower spine as they stepped over him, and he winced as a fresh wave of pain tore through his body. All around was panic — screams, yells for help, and hysteria as smoke filled the dining room. He coughed, hurting even more.

"Watch what you're doing," he bellowed as a man's foot narrowly missed his face. He had to get up from the floor. In their terror, the other guests were oblivious to his plight. They would trample him underfoot if he didn't move. He struggled into a sitting position. The pain in his back seemed less — maybe it was only numb — but he dragged himself against the wall. At least he was out of the main throughfare.

There was a bottleneck at the front door as people jostled and shoved, all reasoning lost to panic.

The fire Dean had started had consumed three tables now. Huge flames licked towards the ceiling. *Shit.* The whole place was about to be destroyed.

Material things could be replaced. A building could be rebuilt, but Rafiq was already dead, and the last he'd seen of Jerico, Dean had been holding the gun on him. He couldn't waste time. He needed to get out of here and find them.

"Andy." Mari rushed towards him out of the smoke, a napkin clutched to her face. Matt was with her.

"Mam! What are you still doing here?"

"I couldn't leave you." She knelt beside him. She stiffened at the sight of the blood on his shirt, but her maternal grit held out. "How bad is it? Where did the bullet hit?"

"Just my shoulder," he said. "I'll live, but not for long unless we can get out of here."

Matt was down at his other side. "Can you stand? If you put your good arm around my shoulder, I'll take your weight."

He had no other option. He gritted his teeth, and when Matt slipped beneath his shoulder and wrapped his arm around his neck, he was ready. On the count of three they rose. The pain in his right shoulder reached a new height. It threatened to overcome him, but as his vision dimmed and a faint approached, he fought against it. No way would he give in, not while Jerico needed him.

As he got fully to his feet, the intensity of the heat and smoke amplified.

People were still jammed in the front door. "We'll never get out that way." He couldn't even see the kitchen entrance for the flames that consumed that entire half of the room. They were trapped.

"Front window," Matt said, coughing. He took Andy's weight as they stumbled towards it. "Mari, get a chair. Smash a way out."

She didn't hesitate. As they approached the front, the same window Dean had launched his petrol bomb through last week, Mari grabbed the back of a dining chair. Displaying strength Andy had no idea she possessed, she raised the chair and swung it in a wide arch. It bounced straight back on her first attempt. She cried in desperation, then heaved the chair again, crashing down with even greater force.

The window burst outwards.

Almost immediately, the heat behind them escalated.

Despite the pain, Andy clung tightener to Matt.

Jake and Arnie appeared at the open window. Jake reached in and grabbed his mother. Mari glanced back to check they were behind her.

"Get out," Andy yelled. "We're right here."

With Jake's help, she climbed up onto the windowsill, and he lifted her down to the street. Arnie was already stretching for Matt and Andy. With his useless shoulder on one side and Matt on the other, Andy couldn't see a way over.

"You go first," he said to Matt. "I'll try to follow you through."

"No," Arnie yelled. "Get your bum up onto the ledge. I'll support you as Matt shoves you over."

There was no time to think of a better way. Andy backed up to the window, hitched his arse onto the sill. The pressure put intense strain on his lower back. He was certain now that his coccyx was broken. It didn't matter. Suddenly Arnie's hands were beneath his shoulders. The pain was blinding, but somehow he dragged him through the gap. Matt lifted Andy's legs and got him over the side, clambering straight through after him.

They staggered away from the window, gasping for clean air.

He was out of danger.

Now all that mattered was finding Jerico.

* * * *

Dean's gun was pressed hard into Jerico's back, to the right of his spine. They were at the bottom of South Bank Terrace, making their way upwards. There were no other people on the route as the road forked away from the town and shops and the bars that lined Pier Street. Smoke from the fire in the restaurant drifted in their direction. Jerico hadn't heard a signal siren yet.

Where were the emergency services? The police, ambulance and fire brigade? Rafiq and Andy had been shot, the building was being destroyed, so where was the help? Rafiq had taken a bullet to the head. There was no chance of survival. Jerico was almost certain the bullet for Andy had gone off target. It had all happened in an instant, but he was sure he'd seen the plume of blood appear on Andy's shoulder before he went down. It was a sliver of hope, but he clung to it. Andy had to make it out of there. Jerico couldn't consider any other possibility.

"What happened to the security people at the back door?" he asked, out of breath as Dean forced him up the hill at a rapid pace.

Scoffing laughter from behind. "Bang-bang."

"You shot them, too? How fucking insane are you?"

"If you haven't figured it out already, you'll learn soon enough."

Grief choked the outrage and anger that had consumed Jerico so far. "You're killing innocent people. For what? Because you lost on a TV show ten years ago? Can't you see how warped that is?"

Dean jabbed the muzzle of the gun into his back. "I didn't lose anything. I was cheated out of it. And that wasn't all. You stole everything—the career and success I should have had, that I deserve."

"Oh, fuck off. That's absolute bullshit. You can't kill people over something you never had. You had plenty of opportunities to start a career afterwards. There are dozens of contestants who've been on the show and didn't win. They still used the experience to their advantage and made the most of it. But you? You chose to wallow in pity and hate and blame everyone else for your inadequacies. You pulled the trigger on those people tonight, and no one else is to blame for that."

"If you don't want me to pull it again right now, you'll shut your lying mouth." He screwed the gun into the soft flesh beneath Jerico's ribs.

Dean intended to kill him, that much was clear, but Jerico wasn't dead yet. Dean had something grander in mind than to shoot him here and leave him on the pavement. Jerico had to use that to his advantage. The longer he stalled the moment of death, the better chance he'd have.

They came upon South Bank Terrace and Andy's house.

Is this where he plans to do it? Jerico couldn't think what significance the place must have. Why would he want to stage his murder here?

"Keep walking," Dean said. "All the way to the top."

So, that's not the plan, then.

"Where the hell are we going? You're nuts, you know? What's got into your crazed brain now?"

"This one is all on you." A note of pride had crept into Dean's voice. "Well, no, the idea was all mine, but you inspired it when you announced this town was to be the venue for your shitty restaurant. I'm thorough in my research. That's how I've been living under your nose the whole time you've been here, and you had no idea until I wanted you to know."

He sounded more insane than ever. *Keep him talking. Humour him. There's still a chance.*

"What's this brilliant idea then. Astound me."

Another scoffing laugh. "When I investigated Nyemouth, one of the top stories I found was about that kid who tried to kill Arnie Walker a few years ago. Fascinating really, how it all started when the boy tried to throw a woman over the edge of a cliff — North Point, over on the other side. It was such a funny idea I wanted to honour it…only it must be different. I have to mix it up a little." He giggled. "Instead of throwing you off North Point, I'm going to chuck you off the cliff up here on South Point instead."

* * * *

Andy sat on the pavement, across the road from Osman's Syrian Kitchen, his legs outstretched. His lower back throbbed, and he did what he could to keep the pressure off it.

Jake unbuttoned his shirt. "Lean forward slightly," he said.

Andy did as he asked, grimacing at the pain. Jake gently peeled the blood-shodden shirt from his skin and leaned in, examining his shoulder. He eased Andy back against the wall and pressed a folded handkerchief to his wound. Andy flinched, then took over. It somehow hurt less when he applied pressure to the bleeding himself.

"How does it look?"

"Could be worse," Jake said. "There's no exit wound at the back, so the bullet is still in there. Thankfully, it's high on your shoulder, so there are no vital organs at risk."

Mari paced the pavement in front of him, her phone pressed to her ear. "I can't even get through. How the hell can there be no answer on an emergency number?"

"Did everyone get out all right?" Andy asked.

"I think so," Jake said. "Matt and Jacob are over there giving first aid to the injured. I think the restaurant is clear. Everyone is away from the doors. But I don't know why it's taking so long for help to arrive?"

"We need to find Jerico." Andy bent his knees, and using the wall behind him for support, he shuffled to his feet.

"I don't think that's a good idea." Jake put a hand on his good shoulder. "You need to rest."

He shook his head. "I need Jerico. Did anyone see where they went?"

Where would Dean have taken him? Andy didn't have a clue. No one even knew where he'd been hiding all this time, let alone what he might have planned. He couldn't lose Jerico now, not after all the years they'd missed being together.

Arnie Walker dashed across the street towards them, wide eyed. He had his phone to his ear. There was an urgency about his manner.

"What is it?" Andy demanded. One word of bad news would break him.

"It's Dominic. He's gone after them — Jerico and that nut."

Andy stiffened. "Where are they?"

Arnie pointed. "They're up on South Bank. He says they're heading for the point."

Adrenaline rushed through Andy's body. A sense of raw urgency surmounted all his pain. Without a thought for himself, he hurried for the bank.

Chapter Twenty-Five

By the time they reached the top of the cliff, the evening sky was a deepening shade, somewhere between cobalt and navy blue. This far north, in the height of summer, darkness was a long way off. They hadn't spoken for several minutes. Jerico conserved his energy. If he was going to delay the inevitable, he'd need all his reserves to trigger and unsettle Dean.

He could no longer smell the fire, and neither could he hear a single siren. They were far above the town now, and he prayed that help had arrived. It might not do him much good — he doubted anyone had seen him leave with Dean — but he had to believe Andy and the people in the restaurant were safe.

"Right," Dean said. "We can stop here." He wheezed, out of breath,

They were at the highest peak of South Point. A little over a week ago, he'd enjoyed an evening walk along this cliff with Andy. They'd been so happy, caught up in each other and the gorgeous view, and they had rekindled their romance. How shitty to be up here again with the man who had spent the last ten years trying to destroy him. Now tonight, the bastard was going to succeed.

No way I'm giving in. He won't take me without a fight.

Chilled, salty air blew in from the sea. Jerico inhaled deeply, fortifying himself. The water offshore was the choppiest he had seen it in days. It was a beautiful sight. He hoped it would not be one of the last things he ever saw.

"You must have enjoyed it," he said, throwing a backwards look to Dean.

Dean had moved several metres away. He was unfocused, gasping for breath. His gun hand trembled, though it remained fixed on Jerico. If the trigger went off, he'd be dead.

"What? Burning your business to the ground? Shooting your friend? Your new fella? Yes, I enjoyed all of it."

Keep it together. He's losing it. You need to stay calm.

"No...prison."

Dean's lips quavered. "The fuck you talking about?"

"It seems to me that you must have enjoyed your time inside, so much that you want to spend the rest of your life there."

His skin flushed puce. "Enjoyed it? *You're* the one who put me there. What the fuck are you talking about?"

"It's true. After what you've done tonight, I doubt they'll ever let you out again."

Dean sucked an angry breath through his teeth. He jabbed the gun towards Jerico. "You know how I got through it, twenty months inside, eh? By thinking of all the ways I was going to get back at you. There's a lot of time to think when you're inside — and plenty of internet access too. As long as you're not searching for porn, no one gives a shit what you're looking at. I kept tabs on you...all your social media posts, living like a fucking king while I festered in there. And I thought of all the things I would do to you when I got out."

He paced back and forward, agitated, while keeping the gun on Jerico. Jerico had touched a nerve. Dean was disconcerted, becoming more frantic.

"*Enjoyed fucking prison,*" he yelled. "You piece of *shit*. The things I had to do to just survive in there, especially in the beginning. Do you have any idea what it was like for a cute boy like me, who had never been inside before? 'Fresh meat', that's what they called me. And I couldn't retaliate. Couldn't do anything to fuck up my chances of an early release. I wasn't going to spend a minute longer than I had to in there, because I needed to be out if I was ever going to get even with you."

Jerico kept his voice calm and measured. "You didn't have to do any of it. Didn't you realise the misery you'd caused me already? What those years of abuse and torment had done? You'd already hurt me deeply, but you were too wound up in jealousy and spite to ever see it."

"No way. That's not enough. It's *never* enough. You don't know the first thing about suffering."

"I do. Everybody does. We all go through it. We deal with it more efficiently than starting fires and shooting people."

"Shut up," he screamed, baring his teeth. *A rabid wolf.*

"Dean, please." Soft voice, trying to reason. "There's a better way than this."

Dean shook his head and seemed to bring his mania into focus. A calmness came over him. Jerico looked into his eyes and saw nothing, just a dead stare.

Dean's gun hand was as steady as an assassin's. "You're right. There is another way. And it's right off the edge of that cliff."

* * * *

Arnie and Jake caught up with Andy as he hurried up South Bank Terrace.

"You've been shot. You can't do this," Jake said, drawing alongside him.

Andy didn't slow down. He clutched the bloody handkerchief to this shoulder and contended with the pain. He would *not* leave Jerico on his own with that madman.

"Andy, please," Jake pleaded. "You're in a bad way."

"I have to reach him," he said, climbing the bank with determined focus.

"He's right," Arnie said. "Jake, you know better than anyone what it's like when the man you love is in danger." He leaned into Andy's good side, putting a strong arm around him. "We're with you, too. You don't have to do this alone." Arnie held his phone in his other hand, he brought it to his ear and listened. Dominic was still following Jerico and Dean.

"Can he see them?" Andy asked.

After a moment Arnie said, "They're up on the point now." He paused, listening. "Okay, we're on our way. Andy wouldn't take no for an answer."

Jake continued to try the emergency services with his own phone. "Shit. Still engaged. What the hell is going on? This night is a fucking disaster, and the police won't even answer the phone."

"Try social media," Andy told him. "There's a Nyemouth Police page. See if you can raise an alarm on there."

Jake tapped his phone as they hurried upwards. Andy found it difficult to breath on the incline but would not be stopped. They came upon his house. If only he was safely tucked up in there with Jerico, and tonight was nothing but a bad dream. As he glanced to the window, he saw Patches looking out, a worried expression on his face. The cat's mouth opened as he meowed to his companion from behind the glass.

"There's been an incident on the other side of the river," Jake said, scrolling through his phone. "Serious injuries...it happened about seven o'clock...but the cops know about the restaurant. Thank Christ. They are finally on their way."

"Tell them to get someone up to South Point," Arnie said. "Tell them the man responsible for it all is up there, armed and dangerous."

Jake was already keying in the information.

They reached the end of the terrace. The bank became steeper as it veered to the right. Arnie gripped him tighter as they staggered over uneven terrain.

Ahead of them was Dominic. He crouched behind a grassy mound. He turned as he heard them approach and shook his hand, urging them to keep quiet. They dropped to the ground beside him.

Dominic pointed. "Over there. He hasn't seen me yet."

Andy raised his head above the embankment. Jerico and Dean were about forty yards away, less than a few metres from the edge of the cliff. Jerico's hands were raised. He spoke to Dean, though the distance and the breeze prevented Andy from hearing what was said.

"What's he doing?" he whispered.

"I think Jerico is trying to talk him around," Dominic whispered back. He was calm and deathly serious. Andy remembered that before Dominic had retired to Nyemouth, become an author and joined the lifeboat crew, he'd been in the Royal Marines. If there was a good man to have on his side right now, Dominic was it.

Desperation and helplessness were all-consuming. "I need to get over there," Andy moaned. "I want to be with him."

"No," Dominic said firmly. "He's shot you once already. If he thinks you're alive, he'll finish you off for good. Jerico is doing a good job at keeping him calm. The best thing to do for now is let him continue."

Time was running short. Dean's entire body language and expression had changed. Jerico had only managed to unsettle him so far, but he had snapped back into focus. The cunning and composure that had gotten Dean here was in control again. As Dean came towards him, Jerico took a reluctant step backwards. He glanced behind and saw the edge of the cliff was less than fifteen feet away.

Shit.

"Is this how you want to be remembered?" he asked, giving it one last go. "Yeah, you left *Top Cook* earlier than you wanted, but viewers loved you. They still remember you."

"I know how they remember me. I've seen the clips on *When TV Goes Horribly Wrong*, and *Reality TV's Most Disastrous Moments*. I'm a laughingstock in the media."

"You didn't have to be. You could have turned it around, proved them all wrong."

A chilling smile. "I'm doing that right now. After tonight, Dean Ferguson will no longer be thought of a joke. Nobody will laugh when they talk about me again."

"You'll be remembered for killing people, for cold-blooded murder. I'm damn sure I'd rather be known as a runner-up in a cookery competition than for that. Jesus, Dean, come on. Just think about it for a minute."

Another step closer for Dean. Jerico moved backwards.

"I've done nothing else but think about it, you dumb fuck. Have you not listened to a single word I've said? All this, tonight, didn't just happen."

"You do know you'll never get away with it. They'll catch you, and you won't get out this time. You'll spend the rest of your life in prison."

Dean pulled the trigger.

A patch of earth exploded inches from Jerico's left foot. He staggered backwards.

Dean laughed. "Your face. I wish I could get my camera out. Actually, that's something I *should* have thought of—one of those bodycam things so I could record all this. I guess I'll have to make do with the memories."

He fired again, just missing Jerico's right foot. Jerico leapt and staggered closer to the cliff edge.

Oh fuck. There was no reasoning with him now. *This is it...almost over.*

Jerico felt a strange sense of unreality. For a second he was outside of his body, watching a movie. Only this is the part where the hero would do something brilliant and stop the villain. Life was no movie. The gun was real, and the mad man before him was a killer rather than an actor.

His mind flashed on Andy. *Please be okay. Go on to live a happy life. I wish we could have had more time together but I'm grateful for knowing you, for loving you again these last few days.*

"At last, you're moving in the right direction," Dean said. He came closer. "Keep going. Over the side with you." A crazed giggled.

"No fucking way. If you want to kill me, you'll have to do it yourself."

Dean lashed forward with the gun, sending Jerico closer to the precipice. He became aware of the sea, the booming sound of the waves on the rocks below. It all seemed amplified. When he had looked before, the water had been relatively okay. Now it sounded like a storm was raging down there.

He risked a look behind. He was four feet from the edge.

When Dean fired again, Jerico flinched but didn't move.

"You're gonna have to shoot me, if you've got the balls to do it," he yelled. "Come on, you worthless, talentless fuck." Jerico banged his fists against his chest.

Dean raised the gun and pointed directly at him. "You've always underestimated me. I'm gonna enjoy this."

He pulled the trigger.

The hollow click of an empty weapon.

Jerico seized the moment, and leapt at Dean, but Dean was already launching himself at Jerico.

They collided. Jerico got two strong punches into Dean's torso before they hit the ground. Dean was an animal. He kicked and writhed. His clawed fingers targeted Jerico's eyes. Jerico kept his head clear, trying to control Dean with his greater weight, but it was like holding on to a snake.

Dean twisted, struggled. They rolled over.

And over.

Jerico realised too late the direction they were heading.

In the next moment there was no ground beneath them at all as they tumbled over the edge of the cliff.

Chapter Twenty-Six

The instant Dean pulled the trigger on an empty gun, Dominic sprang to his feet and ran towards them. Despite his injuries, Andy was right behind him. They had him outnumbered. Out of bullets, Dean wouldn't stand a chance. As he raced forward, it looked like Jerico already had an advantage over him. Jerico was much bigger and stronger. Andy hoped he'd have beaten seven shades of shit out of him before they even got there.

But as they rolled towards the edge, he had a sickening foreboding of what was about to happen. It was like watching a spilled glass roll to the end of a table, not being able to reach it until it was too late.

And suddenly it was too late.

Jerico and Dean went over the cliff.

Andy screamed in outrage and pain. He didn't stop running.

Dominic reached the edge and dropped to his knees, crawling forward. Andy fell beside him, scrabbling to see over, terrified of what he would find.

Then there was a flash of hope.

Jerico was there. He clung to a small fissure in the cliff face, about four feet from the top. His knuckles were white. His face twisted, baring his teeth as he fought to hold on. About fifteen feet below Jerico, Dean had landed on a narrow outcrop. It was no more than a few inches, but the bastard was in a far safer position than Jerico was. If he lost his grip, the jagged rocks spelled disaster two hundred feet below.

"Jerico," he called. "Hang on. Don't let go. We'll get you. Honey, we're going to get you up." He turned to Dominic. "What can we do?"

Dominic reared back onto his knees. Arnie and Jake had reached them, too. They gazed over the edge, their eyes wide with fear.

Dominic unbuckled his belt and tore it out of his trousers. "Your belts. I need them all, if they're strong enough. Leather is best."

They obeyed without question. Taking off their belts and handing them over. Dominic re-buckled his own into a loop, then linked it with Andy's, before joining it to Arnie's and Jake's.

"Will it be strong enough to hold his weight?" Andy shivered with anxiety.

"I hope so. The leather is strong enough. I just hope the fastenings are, too."

Please, God, help us to save him.

"I'll need help," Dominic said. "It's a lot of weight to bear. When I'm in position, Arnie, put all your own weight on my right leg. Jake, you take the left. Got it?"

They nodded.

"Okay." Dominic got on his belly and crawled to the edge. He hooked one of the belt loops around his elbow and threw the rest over the side.

Jerico's prayers were answered when he heard Andy's voice and looked up to see him. He was alive. That fact alone made Jerico determined to survive. The fissure in the rock face that he clung to was barely three inches deep. His fingers had the most precarious hold. His toes, pushed against the rock, had little more than indents to steady against.

But Andy was alive.

Despite clinging to a cliff edge, a few hundred feet from sure death, Jerico experienced a moment of relief and gratitude.

"Let go." Dean's voice rose from below.

So, he had survived the fall, too. Jerico was not going to risk his own insecure position to look down and find out where he was.

"Let go, you bastard. I want to see you smashed all over those rocks. Don't deny me that."

Jerico ignored the voice of the devil from below and kept his focus upwards, towards hope.

Andy's face appeared again and another man. It was Dominic Melton.

Dominic leaned farther out and lowered something down to him. It brushed against the rock beside him. Jerico slowly turned his head to look — a dark leather belt.

"Can you grab onto it?" Dominic called down.

Jerico didn't know. Reaching for the lifeline would mean letting go of the ridge. Could he do it fast enough to avoid a catastrophic fall?

"Just let go, you fucker. Fucking die, won't you?"

The pure hatred coming from Dean gave him a boost. Maybe he would plunge to his death and maybe he wouldn't. And what could be better revenge against Dean than getting out of this alive?

"Come on," Andy pleaded from above. "Grab the belts. It's the only way."

Jerico's heart was in his throat. His mouth was dry. He had never been more terrified.

This was his only chance of being with Andy again.

His breathing was shallow. He forced himself to take deeper, slower breaths.

One. Two. Three.

He pressed his feet as hard as he could against the rock for stability and let go with his right hand.

He caught the belt loop and instinctively wrapped it around his elbow, before pulling it tight to his body. He still gripped the fissure with his left hand.

"Can you pull yourself up?" Dominic asked.

"I…I'll try."

Jerico had no experience of rock climbing. He had no real head for heights to ever consider such an activity as leisure.

Take your time. Think.

With the belt looped around his elbow, he slowly wound it all around his right forearm, and on another breath, he let go of his purchase on the rock and grabbed a position higher up the belt. The leather and its metal buckles creaked. Would this thing even hold him? Another deep breath and he pushed with his feet, before making a grab for a higher position on the belt chain.

"That's it," Andy said. "Keep going."

Jerico pressed himself flat against the cliff, taking more deep breaths, before repeating the manoeuvre…a push through his legs, then a climb of the belt.

"*Fall, you bastard. Faaaaallll.*" Dean's screams were the sound of a nightmare.

"Ignore him. Come to me. You're almost there. Just a few more feet."

Jerico was close to exhaustion. With Andy's voice as his beacon, he summoned his last reserve of strength and pushed again. This time, as he rose, he came face to face with Dominic's determined features. Then there were hands reaching down for him. Arnie Walker leaned over the edge and grabbed the waist of Jerico's trousers. With astonishing strength, Arnie hauled him up and over, and he was lying on flat ground again.

Jerico gasped for breath. He had made it.

Then Andy was above him, bending over and kissing him. "Oh my God, I thought I'd lost you."

The right side of Andy's shirt was covered with blood from neck to waist and all down the arm. Jerico pushed into a sitting position. "What…? So much blood. Are you all right?"

"It's only my shoulder," Andy said, kissing him again. "I'll live."

Jerico carefully wrapped his arm around Andy's good side. It was wonderful to hold him. They had come so close to losing each other. He'd never let that happen again.

"It won't reach him," he heard Dominic say from behind.

Jerico turned. Dominic and Arnie were on their bellies again, draping the belt-rope over the side of the cliff again.

"He's too far down," Arnie said.

Jerico looked at Andy for an explanation.

"Dean," he said. "He's on a ledge, farther down."

Jerico struggled to his feet. "How far?"

"A good twenty feet," Dominic said.

"I've got a belt too," Jerico said. "If I add to yours, will it be long enough?"

"No. It was only enough to reach you. We'd need another five belts to get that far. Even then, I'm not sure it would bear the weight of pulling him all that way."

"We need to get him up," Jerico said. "That man is going to face the consequences of what he's done tonight. He's going to prison for the rest of his life."

Arnie was still on his front, looking over. "I think he'll be okay. He's on a ledge. It's a lot more secure than where you were."

Dominic pulled out his phone. "I'll get onto the coastguard. They'll be able to reach him with a helicopter and a winch. Talk to him, will you? Keep him calm."

Dominic wandered off to make his call, while Arnie shouted reassurances down to Dean.

"It seems more than he deserves," Andy said, leaning against Jerico.

"Hey, you're freezing." Andy's skin was like ice. Jerico pulled him to his chest, wrapping him in his arms for warmth. "You need to go to the hospital."

"I need you," he replied, resting his head on Jerico's shoulder.

"Thank God," Jake suddenly said.

They all looked up at the sound of approaching sirens.

"Finally," Jerico muttered.

Jake ran towards the road, waving to draw the attention of the approaching rescue services.

"Maybe they'll have something to get him up," Andy said, nodding to the cliff edge.

"Hopefully. And once they do, they can take my statement and ensure he's never a danger to a member of the public again."

They stepped closer to the verge.

"How is he doing?" Jerico asked. He leaned over. Dean was on a tiny ledge. The drop beneath him was sickening. He hadn't appreciated just how far it was when he was hanging there himself.

"He hasn't said a word," Arnie told him. "But he seems calm enough. He'll be okay if he stays where he is." He cupped his hands over his mouth and called down. "Help has just arrived. Hang in there. It won't be long. They'll get you up."

Dean looked up, and his eyes locked with Jerico's. A black storm passed across his face. Then he turned his head from left to right, searching. He flattened his hands against the rock and shuffled across.

"What's he doing?" Andy gasped.

"He's trying to make a run for it," Jerico said.

"Stay where you are," Arnie shouted. "Just keep still."

Dean movements were frantic. He shifted farther across the ledge. There was nowhere for him to go.

"Just wait," Jerico yelled. "You can't get away. Wait for help."

Dean snapped his head upwards. His expression was feral. Even in this perilous position, his hatred for Jerico burned through his eyes. He shuffled farther to the right.

Jerico knew where this was leading. Holding on to Andy, he stepped back from the edge.

Seconds later a lamentable scream, loud before falling away, brought ten years of torment to an end.

Epilogue

Four months later

Jerico stood in the kitchen of Andy's house stirring a pot of lamb meatballs in sauce. They were Andy's current favourite. It was not yet five o'clock, but it was already dark. The lights inside were all on, creating a warm, cosy atmosphere. Andy would be home from work soon, and Jerico wanted to have dinner ready for him.

Patches sat on one of the dining room chairs, watching him with an inquisitively tilted head.

"Too spicy for you, handsome boy. You can have your dinner as soon as daddy gets in."

Jerico grabbed another pan from the cupboard and filled it with water, setting it to boil to make a bulgar wheat side to accompany the meatballs. He'd been living with Andy since the night in June when they had both looked death in the face. Though the house was small, it was perfect for the three of them. Thankfully,

Patches had made him feel as welcome as Andy had in his home.

Most days Jerico divided his time between here and the restaurant just a short walk down the hill. The fire had destroyed the interior, but the old Grade II-listed building had stood firm. It had taken a team of eight men almost two months to gut the fire-damaged insides and get the venue back to a condition where he could start again. Together with a designer and his new business partner Arnie Walker, Jerico had worked day and night to create a new vision from the destruction Dean had caused. In one month from now, Nyemouth would witness the opening of a new specialist restaurant, Rafiq's Syrian Kitchen.

Rafiq had lost his life in that very building. It seemed only fitting that it would carry his name into the future. Rafiq's family had been integral to the new venture, and together with Jerico had created a menu that featured all his favourite dishes. Jerico was determined that the name Rafiq Sultan would become part of Nyemouth history and would be remembered long after Dean Ferguson had been forgotten.

He heard the front gate opening. Patches perked up, too, turning to stare at the front door. Seconds later it opened, and Andy walked in, looking stylish and handsome in his work suit. Jerico grabbed a towel to wipe his hands and hurried forward to greet Andy with a kiss on the lips.

"Welcome home."

"Mmm." Andy kissed him back. "It's good to be home."

Since returning to work at the start of September, Andy had adjusted his work-homelife balance. Twelve-hour days were a thing of the past. He even made time for a full lunch hour to catch up with Jerico each day. Andy hadn't fully recovered from the injuries he had sustained. The bullet had been removed from his shoulder, but he required regular physio to repair the damage it had done and manage the pain, and the doctors had warned that his broken coccyx could take anything between six months to a year to heal. There was no rushing these things, and Jerico was there as much as possible to make sure Andy took it easy.

They went into the kitchen, and Patches leapt down to greet Andy. Andy picked him up and rested him on his good shoulder, kissing the top of the cat's purring head. "I've missed you, too," he said, nuzzling into fur. "I hope you've had a lovely day."

Jerico's heart swelled. He'd spent the best part of two decades travelling the world, a nomad moving from job to job. This was the first place that had ever felt like home. In this little house, above the crazy town, with the man he loved and his adorable old cat.

"Why don't I feed him while you change?" he suggested. "Then we can eat before going out."

Andy gave Patches another kiss, then a second for Jerico, before hurrying upstairs.

Jerico rooted through the cupboard, looking at the pouches of cat food. Patches hurried over, brushing against his leg, clearly impatient.

"Seeing as we're having lamb, I think it's only fair that you do, too." He tore into one of the sachets and spooned it into a bowl to much excitement from Patches.

The table was already set. He lit the four candles he had put out earlier. They created even greater warmth to the already cosy room. After a glorious summer, he'd been surprised at how quickly autumn had descended upon Nyemouth. And since the clocks had been set back on daylight saving time last weekend, the evenings had gotten very dark, very early.

All the better to snuggle up with Andy for a perfect evening on the sofa watching TV.

But not tonight.

He judged from the sounds on the creaky old floor above when Andy was almost ready, and Jerico set out their meal. There were warm flatbreads and cold beer to accompany the meat balls. The food was steaming on the table when Andy came back downstairs, looking casual and sexy in a pair of jeans, a blue shirt and a woollen, navy sweater.

"Smells good," he said, taking a seat. Andy went straight for the bread. He tore off a strip and mopped up some of the spicy sauce. "And it tastes even better."

Jerico took the seat beside him. He wanted to make the most of the next few weeks. Once the restaurant opened, he'd be lucky if he was home for dinner once or twice a week, but until then, he was going to enjoy it.

"How was your mum today?" he asked.

Andy chewed and swallowed. "She's fine. She was on a half day, so I didn't see much of her."

Since the attack, Mari and her fiancé Richie had become a cherished part of Jerico's newfound family. Richie had been lucky. Despite sustaining a direct gunshot wound to the chest, the protective vest he wore as part of his uniform had taken the brunt of the bullet. Though he'd sustained major bruising from the close impact, Richie had survived. Sophia, one of his security officers, had also taken a hit and lived to tell the tale. Though Rafiq had lost his life that night, the fatalities could have been so much worse.

Three people had been injured in the crash Dean had caused as a diversion earlier in the evening. He'd driven a stolen car into a group who had been waiting at a bus stop on North Point. A woman in her forties had suffered a broken leg, while two others survived with minor injuries. Several others had been injured while trying to escape the fire at the restaurant.

The only other person to lose their life because of Dean's revenge plot had been Dean himself. The fall from South Point to the jagged rocks below had been too much. When the coastguard had recovered his body, they'd declared that no one could have survived a fall from that height. Jerico had expected to feel some kind of sympathy for him. What enfolded had been a tragedy, but the costs had been too great. He might have felt sorry for Dean if Rafiq was still alive, but given the facts, Jerico's tears had been saved solely for his good friend.

"Will Mari be there tonight?" Jerico asked.

Andy nodded. "Richie's coming, too. I think everyone is."

"Then we should hurry up. I don't want to miss it."

* * * *

The large folding front doors of Nyemouth lifeboat station had been fully opened, and the lifeboat had been moved farther along the marina to make space for the Halloween fundraiser. Inside, the space was taken up with tables selling souvenirs, craft work, tea, coffee and home-made cakes. Volunteers dressed as witches, mummies and zombies handed out sweets and chocolates to the kids out trick-or-treating. For adults, there was a small tent to the side of the station selling beer, spirits and cocktails.

There were almost as many people in the harbour as in the height of summer. The atmosphere was palpable.

"Do they do this every year?" Jerico asked, gazing in wonder at the happy faces around him.

"Yeah," Andy answered. "When I was kid, they used to do a big fundraiser for Guy Fawkes night and have a bonfire and fireworks down on the beach. But a lot of the lifeboat stations along the coast do something similar, so they switched it up here to celebrate Halloween instead."

One of the local tourist boats had entered into the spirit. *Absent Friends*, which usually ran sightseeing trips along the coast during the summer, had been decorated for Halloween. Harry Renner, the handsome skipper, was dressed as a pirate, while his boyfriend Christian wore a Dracula outfit. Together they were running the boat from the marina out past the piers and back, with all the proceeds going to the lifeboat charity.

"We should do that," Jerico said, pointing at the boat as it glided along the river. "A cruise for old times."

Andy laughed. "It's not quite the luxury cruise ships we were used to."

"No," Jerico said, taking his hand. "It looks even better."

"Let's get a hot drink first. I need to warm up before we go out on the water."

After the scorching temperatures of summer, things were a whole lot colder in late October. Jerico didn't mind. He was excited to discover all the changes the seasons brought about in this area of the world. He'd fallen in love with Nyemouth and wanted to experience every part of it.

As they headed for the station, he spotted Arnie and Dominic and Matt and Jake walking along the harbour walls with collection buckets. Arnie looked up, catching his eye, and they waved. Jerico would always be indebted to those guys. They had saved his life without a thought for their own safety. As lifeboat volunteers, Jake and Dominic were already hailed as local heroes, but as far as Jerico was concerned, they all were. In the last few months, they had become great friends, and now Arnie was also his business partner. After Rafiq, Jerico had been prepared to continue on his own, but when Arnie had made an offer to help him rebuild, he was the only man he could imagine doing it with.

The interior of the station was warmer than outside, but with the front doors open, a chill circulated from the river. They queued up at the refreshment stall to find Jacob behind the counter, serving the teas.

"How's it going?" Andy asked.

"Marvellous," Jacob answered. "I think we're well on the way to beating last year's total."

He handed them their drinks, and Jerico slipped him a twenty-pound note.

"Let me get your change," Jacob said, rooting through a cash tin.

"No," Jerico insisted. "Keep it. It's worth every penny."

They huddled around an electric heater and sipped their hot drinks.

"I love it here," Jerico said.

"I can tell. You haven't stopped grinning since we arrived."

"That obvious?"

"Very. But it's sweet...and much appreciated. This whole service runs on charity contributions, so they need every penny."

"Maybe I can do something for the next event. Once the restaurant is open, we could host a fundraiser."

"A brilliant idea." Andy leaned over and kissed him. "You're full of them, Mr. Osman."

"I'm inspired, that's all." Jerico kissed him back. "By you."

From there, they bought tickets for the boat trip and queued up at the dock.

"We should have worn costumes," Andy said, pointing out that everyone else in the line was dressed up.

"There's always next year. We can start planning our looks when we get home."

When the boat was ready, they boarded and settled into their seats in stern. Jerico slipped his arm around Andy's waist, pulling him close as *Absent Friends* moved slowly along the river. The town was even more beautiful from this angle, looking up at it from the water. They had left a light on at home before coming down, and he could even make out the house from here.

As they approached the piers and the entrance to the sea, the wind became even more biting. They huddled closer together for warmth, but it was only his limbs that were cold. Inside, his heart and his soul were warm. Jerico Osman was the luckiest man in the world. He'd been given a second chance with the man he loved and found peace in a place he adored.

He hugged Andy tighter and inhaled deeply. He had everything he'd ever wanted, and nothing in the world could beat that.

Want to see more from this author? Here's a taster for you to enjoy!

Basic Instincts: Night Crimes
Thom Collins

Excerpt

It was dark when Kurtis Langham arrived in the centre of Blyham. Though he was a stranger to the city, the navigation app on his phone had made easy work of the side streets once he came off the ring road, and he made it to the car park that had been recommended to him in good time. Eight-twenty on Friday evening and the streets were busy with crowds of young men and women out for a good time. He knew Blyham had a reputation for being a party town, drawing hordes of hen and stag parties each weekend. Tonight appeared to be no exception, and he'd had to drive carefully, as the revellers wandered carelessly into the road.

Kurtis managed to secure a spot on the ground floor of the multi-storey car park, directly beneath a security light and close to a CCTV camera. In recent years, Blyham had also earnt a reputation for anti-social behaviour, violence, homophobia and all-round hate-crime. He was only here for the night and would not take any chances. Get in, do the job and get straight back out. If the traffic was as light as it had been getting here, he could be home in Leeds by one-thirty at the latest.

Kurtis gathered his guitar and microphone from the boot. The booking agent had assured him the venue would have all the sound equipment he would need. He could plug in and play as soon as he arrived. The front entrance of the car park opened onto the city's waterfront area. He heard the beat of competing venues before he reached the street — the dull, heavy thump of loud dance music.

Like in a lot of riverside cities, the waterfront area seemed to have gone through a redevelopment and gentrification programme in the last ten years. He spotted a load of familiar chain bars — the usual suspects that dominated town centres up and down the country, with their expansive glass fronts and self-important door staff. The queues to get inside were huge. He wondered, not for the first time, why anyone would want to waste their nights in such overcrowded, noisy venues.

Kurtis switched the function on his phone app from 'drive' to 'walk'. It took a few seconds to recalculate before informing him that The Blue Pearl was approximately seven minutes away. He set off at a brisk pace. He wished he'd been able to park somewhere closer. The atmosphere was friendly enough right now, but he knew what to expect later in the night, with the stag-party bros who had been drinking heavily all day. Things could turn mean in a matter of seconds.

He hated these weekend townie gigs. There was always an edge to them that he didn't find in the indie bars and student clubs. Many of these guys became arseholes after a few pints. He hoped his luck held out and he could make his way back to the car without incident at the end of the night.

He'd never heard of The Blue Pearl until five-thirty that afternoon. His agent, Roaul, had called as he was getting home from work.

"I've got you a gig tonight in Blyham, if you can get there in time," Roaul had told him. "Their regular guy has left them in the lurch, and it sounds like your kind of thing. It's a monthly themed night—Brit pop, all that old nineties stuff you love, and a load of covers. You could do it in your sleep."

Within twenty minutes, Kurtis had ditched his work suit, showered, changed into jeans and a vintage Bowie T-shirt, loaded the car and got on the road. Other than a gig in Sunderland on Saturday night, he had nothing else planned for the weekend. It would have been nice to have had a couple of hours to plan a set list, but Roaul was right. This was as basic as it got, and he'd be able to program his backing tracks as he went along. It was a piece of piss.

He'd been told to ask for the manager, Zand Riley, when he arrived. They wanted someone to play three sets between nine and midnight. Given the time now, Kurtis doubted he'd be ready to start by then, but they would get good value from him tonight.

Four minutes, straight ahead, directed the navigation app.

Kurtis passed in front of a massive pub with a huge outdoor terrace. It amazed him how many people were standing around outside. It was late September, and the summer was truly over. Though not the coldest of nights, the breeze from the river was fairly biting, and he wouldn't have chosen to spend much time outside, especially given the noise. A group of women screamed in drunken hilarity. He quickened his step.

The people he saw on the street were typical Friday-nighters. The majority of women wore tight, short dresses with lots of make-up and hair pieces. The men were overly tanned, some with muscles and others with beer bellies. Their dress shirts were straight from a packet and some still displayed the creases across the chest and shoulders.

As he kept walking, he became aware of a disturbance ahead.

"So, have you had your cock chopped off yet?" a loud, obnoxious voice hollered, followed by roars of laughter.

A young person, slightly built and wearing a black skirt and pink Converse shoes, was being harassed by four pissed-up arseholes. The boorish men were all older, and bigger, but obviously felt brave because of their number. The young person kept their head down, tried to walk away and mind their own business, but those fuckwits wouldn't allow them past. They were intent on having their fun.

"Have you got it tucked up your arse?" another of the men asked, blocking the path. "I've heard that's what they do," he continued, playing to his audience. "They strap their cocks between their legs and shove it up there."

Their victim made a comment Kurtis couldn't catch before trying to step around. Like basic school-yard bullies, they circled closer, getting in their personal space.

Kurtis clenched his jaw in anger. He hated thugs like these. They were one of the main reasons he avoided city centres on weekend evenings. The innocent didn't have to look far for trouble. It sought them out.

The altercation turned physical as one of the men put his hand on the young person's shoulder to stop them getting away.

"Fucking pricks," he muttered under his breath. Then he yelled, "Hey. The police are on their way."

The four men froze, then turned in his direction. They'd obviously had a lot to drink already. Their actions were slow and fuzzy. The guy who was obviously their alpha-arsehole stepped forward, shrugging his shoulders. "What's the matter?" he asked, a shit-eating grin on his face. "We're not doing anything. It's just banter, that's all."

The young person took advantage of the distraction and hurried away. Kurtis watched as they rushed around the corner and out of sight.

"Just thought you'd want to know," Kurtis said, heading onwards himself. "You know what coppers are like."

The men grumbled among each other. He heard one of them say, "Hey, the fairy's fucked off anyway."

Then another said, "I don't see any cops. Where they supposed to be?"

"Back there," Kurtis said, quickening his step. "And heading this way."

Their leader, sensing the deception he had played on them, scowled at Kurtis. "And who the fuck are you, mate?" He had a strong Liverpudian accent, full of phlegm on the 'k' sounds.

It was a tight situation. If the four of them came after him, he wouldn't stand a chance. Kurtis was lean and nimble. Any other time he'd be able to outrun them without breaking a sweat, but weighed down with his equipment, he had no hope. He hastened his pace, expecting the mob to close in around him at any moment.

By some miracle, they thought better of it. When he chanced a look over his shoulder, he saw them making their way to the god-awful terraced bar.

Fuck. He exhaled slowly. It was true what he'd heard about Blyham. It was a dangerous, shitty place. It might appear fancy with its bars, restaurants and party-vibes, but there was a meanness running beneath the vibrant pulse. He'd witnessed it himself within minutes of his arrival. He knew there was a large LGBTQ village here, but from what he'd read online and seen on social media, it was no safe haven for the community. People were as likely to be attacked there as that young person had been just a few moments ago.

He hoped he wasn't going to be playing his gig tonight to more pissed-up, intolerant bigots.

Kurtis arrived at The Blue Pearl a few minutes later. His first impression was better than any of the bars he'd passed on the way here. There was a small crowd of people outside, smoking and vaping, but they were a more varied bunch than the stag and hen party crowds he'd encountered so far. There were student types in scruffy jeans and band T-shirts, together with older couples seemingly enjoying a date night with wine and cocktails.

There was a female security officer on the door, though she lacked the surly attitude he was used to at most city centre venues.

"Hi," he said. "I'm here to see Zand Riley. The name's Kurtis Langham. I'm tonight's singer."

"He'll be glad to see you," she said with a welcoming smile. "I think he was starting to panic when you weren't here by eight. Go on in and ask for Zand at the bar."

The interior was big but full of character. In place of the usual chrome and glass surfaces he found in most town centre bars, there was a lot of wood, which softened the sounds from a large crowd. There was a good mix of customers, just like the group outside, with all ages and types represented. The atmosphere was positive and warm, with none of the edge he'd felt back there in the streets.

Maybe Blyham wasn't all bad after all.

Kurtis was making his way to the bar when a handsome man in a red T-shirt and navy jacket stepped forward.

"Please tell me your name is Kurtis," the man said. He was somewhere in his late thirties, with thick, black hair combed back from a beautiful face. The hair was short and faded at the back and sides with cute sideburns. He had light-brown skin, a smooth complexion and a strong nose. His boy-next-door looks were transitioning into sexy DILF. In a few more years he'd be one of the most sought-after daddies in town.

"I am," he replied. "Zand?"

With a charming grin and a sexy curl of his upper lip, the man thrust his hand forward. His grip was dry and firm.

"That's me. I'm so glad to see you. You've dug me out of a real hole."

"Your regular guy has let you down, I understand."

"He dropped us this afternoon for a better-paying gig in Newcastle. I didn't think I would get a good replacement at such short notice. What sets The Blue Pearl apart from the other bars along the waterfront is live music. Take that away, and we're just like the rest of them. The agency told me to listen to some of your online stuff, and I knew you'd fit right in."

Zand showed him where he could set up, giving Kurtis another chance to check him out. He was around the same height as Kurtis, give or take an inch, with a lean build and smart-casual dress sense. *Very professional.* Kurtis wondered what he was like behind the scenes, when he wasn't dressed up like a cool manager.

"Brit pop, indie stuff... That's the brief?"

"That's right. We run different themed nights across the month. Indie is one of our most popular. It's possibly the worst night to be left in the lurch. Our customers are very passionate about their music."

There was a decent-sized stage in the top corner of the room, with speakers already in place. "This looks good to me. It should take about ten minutes to get set up and plugged in. Anything you want me to play, or should I just go with the what the crowd reacts to?"

They agreed on the first five songs Kurtis would open with, and from there Zand gave him freedom to do what he wanted.

"Is this the kind of genre you usually play?" Zand asked.

"I'm pretty adaptable, but guitar and singing are my thing, so this type of music suits me well. I write some of my owns songs, but don't worry. I won't inflict them on your punters tonight."

Zand gave him a wide smile. Most people would say it was dazzling. Kurtis found it hot as fuck. "A couple of originals will go down great. The people who come here are always open to original stuff. I'm sure you'll get a feel for them soon enough."

Kurtis was incredulous. He had not expected that. Most of the places he played insisted on one-hundred-percent covers. "Okay. Thanks. I'll suss them out as I go along."

There was something very sincere about Zand, and Kurtis didn't think it was just because he'd saved his arse by filling in at short notice. He seemed genuinely interested when Kurtis told him about his music. He even lent a hand, getting him set up on the speakers and fetching a stand for his iPad.

"I almost ran into trouble on my way here." Kurtis told about him about the incident he'd witnessed outside.

Zand grimaced and nodded. "Doesn't surprise me. Don't get me wrong, I love this city, but something has gone wrong in the last few years. So many people have such little respect. Race, gender, sexuality…? There's always somebody who's got it in for someone else. It feels like it's getting worse, but when I talk to my friends from Newcastle, Manchester, Birmingham, I realise it's everywhere. It just seems particularly bad in Blyham right now. I'm sorry you had to witness that."

"It's the kid they were harassing I feel sorry for. I hope they're okay. At least they got away."

Zand's face was deadly serious. "I'll go report it to security now. I know the bar you said those guys went into. I'll radio the staff and tell them to look out for them."

Zand was rising in Kurtis' estimation by the minute. *Friendly, considerate and stunningly handsome.* This shitty little city seemed to have some attractions after all.

About the Author

Thom Collins is the author of Closer by Morning, with Pride Publishing. His love of page turning thrillers began at an early age when his mother caught him reading the latest Jackie Collins book and promptly confiscated it, sparking a life-long love of raunchy novels.

Thom has lived in the North East of England his whole life. He grew up in Northumberland and now lives in County Durham with his husband and two cats. He loves all kinds of genre fiction, especially bonkbusters, thrillers, romance and horror. He is also a cookery book addict with far too many titles cluttering his shelves. When not writing he can be found in the kitchen trying out new recipes. He's a keen traveler but with a fear of flying that gets worse with age, but since taking his first cruise in 2013 he realized that sailing is the way to go.

Thom loves to hear from readers. You can find his contact information, website details and author profile page at https://www.firstforromance.com/

PUBLISHING

Sign up for our newsletter and find out about all our romance book releases, eBook sales and promotions, sneak peeks and FREE romance books!